CERRO GRANDE
A Sheriff Lansing Mystery

Books by Micah S. Hackler

Sheriff Lansing Mysteries
Legend of the Dead
Coyote Returns
The Shadow Catcher
The Dark Canyon
The Mutes
The Weeping Woman
Moon of the Blue Mustang
Badlands
Cerro Grande

Coming Soon!
A Sheriff Lansing Mystery
Montezuma's Fire

CERRO GRANDE
A Sheriff Lansing Mystery

Micah S. Hackler

SPEAKING VOLUMES, LLC
NAPLES, FLORIDA
2021

Cerro Grande

ISBN 978-1-64540-580-1

For Bill and Bobbie Riggle

Acknowledgments

My wonderful wife, Olivia, makes my writing life possible. God blessed me by bringing us together. She continually enriches my world, and I will be forever grateful.

At 70, I owe so many people who, over the years, have been important to me for their friendship, guidance and support. Jim Kerstalude, my roommate from college, who calls me every couple of weeks, so we keep up with each other. Bill Rambin, one of my oldest and dearest friends. When I joined the Air Force, his words of wisdom about keeping the military service in perspective saw me through some tough times. He keeps track of me as well.

Dr. John Kobs, my best friend from high school, reminds me periodically that time and distance never dampens a true friendship.

My friends, co-writers, and counselors for decades, I thank George Sewell and Dan Baldwin for making *The Factory* a reality.

Finally, I have to thank Kurt and Erica Mueller along with their fantastic staff at Speaking Volumes for the continued help and support.

Prologue

May 5, 2000; 3:00 a.m.

As Lincoln Baca picked his way down the slope, the growing forest fire crackled behind him. He stopped to pick up his line pack. It made no sense to climb back to the last staging area with such a heavy load, just to pass that same spot again. About to continue down the mountain to join his crew, he heard the conversation, somewhere below him.

No one else was supposed to be on the mountain.

The "voices" grew louder as they climbed the slope, getting closer. The conversation seemed composed of grunts and grumbles.

Baca froze.

Looming in the darkness, nearly on top of him, was a shadow. The creature was huge . . . over eight feet in height. Next to him was a figure seven feet tall. Behind them two smaller shadows followed. All four walked upright on two legs.

In the flickering light of the growing fire, the faces appeared grotesque . . . though strangely human.

Before he could back away, the tallest of the foursome spotted him. He too stopped.

He studied Baca for a long moment, then let out a deep, guttural grunt.

Baca realized the creature was not warning or threatening him. He was merely acknowledging the Pueblo man's presence.

With nothing more to say, the creature continued to lead his family north, away from the fire, toward safety.

Chapter One

Tito Calle turned south off Highway 15 onto County Road 131. The darkened, dusty track paralleled Artiga Creek for almost eight miles. The mechanic's destination was an old, abandoned barn in the Jemez Mountains. That's where he had left his pickup truck.

The body had been problematic. He couldn't just leave the man where he had fallen. It would have been too easy to trace the corpse to him. He had learned from his brother-in-law to use misdirection whenever possible.

Four miles east of the town of Artiga, State Road 554 turned north to El Rito. The dead man found a resting place at the bottom of an arroyo some distance from the highway. If and when the body was found, Calle hoped the assumption would be that whoever dumped the dead man was heading for Taos. Classic misdirection.

Tito's problems, though, were far from over. There was the issue of the stolen paneled truck he was driving and the pilfered property in the back . . . plus he had to be at work in five hours.

Jimmy Clay had planned everything . . . stolen the truck, engineered the heist, made arrangements to fence the goods. He never confided a single detail to Calle.

"Some partner," Tito groused under his breath.

The night was moonless, and the dim headlights of the truck barely lit the road in front of him. So wrapped up in his thoughts, Calle barely saw the two dark figures dart across the road in front of him.

He stomped on the brakes and swerved off the dirt road. The county had recently graded the track and a foot-high berm of scrapings lined either side. The truck bounced mercilessly as it plowed through the mound, each tire hitting separately. The unsecured contents in the back clanged loudly as the metal objects slammed against the truck's sides and each other.

Skidding to a stop in the high desert scrub, Tito grabbed his flashlight and jumped to the ground. He checked the front bumper to make sure he hadn't hit anything . . . Nothing.

Turning his attention to the road, he swung the beam back and forth, looking for what he had seen . . . or thought he saw.

It wasn't a deer or elk. Nothing on four legs. It might have been two men. But who would be wandering around in these high pastures in the middle of the night?

Again, nothing.

"Probably a bear," Calle said out loud.

He saw no point in checking his cargo. If it bounced around, so what? He didn't have time to rearrange everything.

He inspected the turf around the truck, satisfied that getting back on the road would not be an issue. Only a half mile from where the forest started up again, he would be pulling into the decrepit barn in ten minutes.

Once he was back in his truck heading for home, he had to devise a plausible story as to why he was gone most of the night. Linda would ask questions for sure.

Ramona, his sister, would have questions too. Tito resolved to do what he did best . . . play stupid.

Two sets of eyes watched the paneled truck's red taillights disappear into the darkness. When the dust settled, they followed.

Chapter Two

The large patch of blood was smeared across the asphalt.

That's not what Sheriff Cliff Lansing expected to see when he arrived at the scene.

***

Lansing took the call as soon as he got into his jeep. There had been a break-in at the Western Auto. The thieves had targeted the most expensive mag wheels.

He told dispatch he would be there in fifteen minutes. There was no reason to hurry. It would take at least that long for Harry Avila to tally his losses.

"Phil," Lansing asked. "Have they made any progress on the Cerro Grande Fire?"

"Not so much," Phil Peters, the night dispatcher, said. "They just announced the mandatory evacuation of Los Alamos."

"The entire town?"

"Starting at noon."

"Damn," the Sheriff swore.

Six days earlier, Bandelier National Monument attempted a prescribed burn. The fire got out of hand the first night. By Sunday, one hundred firefighters seemed to have the blaze under control.

That night, though, winds picked up from the southwest. Spot fires caused by escaping embers started springing up behind the fire lines.

On Monday, a Type-1 forest fire emergency was declared. The Los Alamos National Laboratory, home of the atomic bomb, was shut down.

By nightfall, three thousand acres had burned, and three hundred and thirty firefighters were on scene.

It was now Wednesday morning. The fire had burned for almost a week and there seemed to be no end in sight. It was started in Sandoval County, quickly jumped to Los Alamos with San Phillipe County just a few miles north.

Lansing could only hope his county and its people would be spared.

***

Avila and Assistant Manager John Gutierrez stood next to chrome-plated mag wheel displays. There was an obvious empty spot where a few selections were taken.

"Morning, Harry," Lansing said, entering through the front door.

Avila looked up from a clipboard. "Oh, hi, Sheriff."

Gutierrez nodded but said nothing.

"What was taken?"

"The SOBs walked off with three complete sets of my rims."

"Were they expensive.?"

"The rims are two hundred and fifty bucks . . . each."

Lansing did a quick calculation. "So, you're looking at three thousand dollars in losses?"

"Yeah," Avila nodded. "And that doesn't include the busted doors. Tack on at least another three, four hundred dollars."

"Don't you have an alarm?"

"Yes. The control panel is in my office. There's a sixty second delay from when the door is opened until the alarm goes off. That gives us plenty of time to shut the system down.

"These jokers knew exactly what to do. After they broke in, they went straight to my office, knocked down the door, then smashed the control panel."

"Can you show me?"

Avila led Lansing first to his office, then to the rear door.

"They did that all in under a minute?"

"Like I said, they knew exactly what to do."

Lansing shook his head. "I'll call Willie Estrada. She'll dust for prints."

"I've contacted the insurance company. They're sending an agent from Segovia. He'll take pictures."

"Can you make sure my office gets copies?"

"Will do, Sheriff."

Lansing stepped outside to inspect the asphalt lot behind the store. Ten feet from the door, he spotted what looked like a large oil stain. The stain didn't appear reddish until he stepped closer.

"Harry."

"Yeah, Sheriff?"

"Is this recent?" He pointed to his discovery.

Harry approached cautiously. "I've never seen it before."

Lansing shook his head. He realized he was probably looking at more than a few stolen rims. Someone had been shot or stabbed and lost a lot of blood.

The body had been dragged through the puddle, smearing a trail.

"Keep everyone away from here," the sheriff ordered.

"Was someone killed?"

"I hope not."

Chapter Three

Lincoln Baca stepped out of his parents' house and looked to the southwest. Smoke billowed into the sky from the Cerro Grande Fire only eight miles away. Black smoke mixed with the white as the fire consumed Los Alamos homes . . . houses that had stood since World War II.

Santa Clara, as well as Segovia caught the drifting smoke. The smell of burning timber permeated everything. The tops of the clouds climbed to 20,000 feet and were blown as far east as the Oklahoma and Texas panhandles . . . even southwest Kansas.

The entire Black Mesa wildlands fire crew was now engaged in the operation. Everyone except for Baca.

***

The 10-man team of wildland firefighters from the Eight Northern Indian Pueblos was positioned at the top of Cerro Grande. Known as the Black Mesa Crew, they had been enlisted to conduct a prescribed burn in Bandelier National Monument. Their fire team chief, Marco Chavarria, thought the exercise would be good training for the less experienced members.

It was going to be a long day. The crew started before noon. The initial rendezvous point was San Juan Pueblo, five miles from Santa Clara.

Chavarria, along with four other firefighters, rode in the F-550 wildfire truck. Lincoln and the rest travelled in a converted school bus.

Twenty firefighters gathered at the Interagency Fire Center on Highway 4, three miles south of Los Alamos. (A twelve-man reserve crew from the park service would join them later.) Besides the Black Mesa Crew there were ten park service firefighters, employees from Bandelier. They all wore the standard yellow, long sleeved, fire resistant NOMEX shirts and green NOMEX pants.

Most had met before. They had fought the Dome Wilderness Fire together four years earlier on the south side of the monument. In fact, the prescribed burn was in response to the lessons learned. The Park Service needed to clear dense undergrowth to prevent future wildfires.

Mike Powers, the Bandelier fire management officer, conducted the briefing at 2:00. Chavarria and Powers soon locked horns. Chavarria cited recent posts from the National Forest Service. Prescribed burns were prohibited due to several wildfires that season.

Powers countered that he operated under the Department of the Interior and National Park Service rules. He had already received approval for the operation. To keep Chavarria satisfied, he would get one final clearance from the weather service before the test fire was started.

Cerro Grande was 10,207-foot-tall with no access roads. The parking area was a thousand feet below the peak. The hike to the top was more than two miles. Each firefighter wore a line pack weighing fifty pounds. Some were heavier. They also carried axes, shovels, and chainsaws.

The intent of the burn was to clear dead brush and trees on the south side of Cerro Grande. The peak was located in the northernmost corner of the park. To the west was Baca Ranch. (The entire area would be renamed Valles Caldera National Wildlife Preserve when the federal government took charge that Summer.) To the northeast was Santa Fe National Forest. Bandelier bordered both.

Once at the summit, the Black Mesa Crew cleared a firebreak for the test fire. At 7:20 Powers ordered ignition. Satisfied with the results, at 8:00 the burn boss directed the prescribed burn to begin.

Using drip torches, Chavarria and his Pueblo firefighters began a "backline" burn down the northeast edge of their zone. The progress was slower than Powers wanted.

Chavarria and Powers clashed a second time. A specific ignition pattern had been outlined during the briefing. On his own initiative, Powers changed the plan.

Reluctantly, the Black Mesa commander ordered his men to follow the new strategy.

By 11:00, Chavarria's fears were coming true. The fire had burned through the backline on the northeast, threatening the national forest. The western edge was burning too fast as it neared Valles Caldera.

The Park Service firefighters were directed to control the fire to the west. The Black Mesa Crew fought the fire along the northeast rim.

By 1:30 a.m. Powers realized the Pueblo men had been working steadily for over ten hours. He had Chavarria send half his men down to the trucks to get some sleep. The reserve crew stepped in to replace them. An hour later, the remaining five men on the Black Mesa crew were ordered down the mountain.

Powers left the mountain as well. The fire was becoming unmanageable. He needed to request additional support . . . from the Forest Service.

Halfway down the slope, Chavarria realized he left his radio at their last position. Lincoln Baca, the youngest member of their crew, volunteered to retrieve the device.

The radio was exactly where his boss said it would be. Lincoln found the raspy conversations annoying and turned the radio off. After the constant noise of pounding axes and whining/grinding chainsaws, the walk down the mountain was pleasantly quiet.

It was after he shouldered his line pack that he had his encounter with the family of strange beasts.

9

What happened next was his own fault.

Once the creatures disappeared into the darkness, Baca wanted to put as much distance between himself and them as quickly as possible. The "quickly" part was his undoing. In his rush, he didn't watch his footing. He tripped and tumbled down the slope for fifty feet.

Something snapped as he slammed into the trunk of a Ponderosa Pine. He tried to push himself up, but the pain in his left arm was debilitating. He let out an involuntary scream . . . then passed out.

Chapter Four

When Lincoln didn't join his comrades at the bus, Chavarria and two other firefighters went to search for him.

All Baca could remember was the excruciating pain when they lifted him to his feet.

They had to cut the straps to his line pack to free him from the load. He barely remembered the rest of the trek down the mountain.

An ambulance took him to the Los Alamos Medical Center.

After cutting away his yellow NOMEX shirt and cotton T, his injury was obvious. His upper left arm was broken.

X-rays confirmed it was a clean break. In addition to the humerus, his collarbone was broken as well. Again, a clean break. The doctor was able to set both bones without surgery.

Baca's cast went from his wrist to his shoulder. It was immobilized, strapped across his stomach to allow his clavicle to mend.

It would be three months before he could resume normal activities.

For an active twenty-one-year-old, three months was an eternity. He would miss most of the forest fire season. He certainly was out of commission for the Cerro Grande Fire.

***

His dog, an animal with a very questionable pedigree, had followed him outside. Chico had been his constant companion since Lincoln was twelve. Baca knelt to give his friend a scratch behind the ears.

"What do you think, boy? Should I have told them what I saw on the mountain?"

Baca had found Chico's favorite spot to be scratched. The dog's back leg furiously pounded the ground.

"You could care less," the fireman grunted. "Just as long as you're fed and watered."

Baca stood when the back door shut. His father approached.

"Your mother and sister are ready to fire their pots," Simon Baca said. "Do you feel like helping?"

"I can try." Anything was better than sitting around doing nothing.

For eighty years Santa Clara Pueblo had been revered for producing some of the best Indian pottery in the southwest. Since the 1950s, buyers from the east coast sought out the work of specific artisans.

Pottery making had always been family traditions. Historically, the craft had been the domain of the women of the household, while the men hunted and worked the fields. Even in modern times, after men started seeking employment outside the pueblo, women still worked the clay, passing on the skills to their daughters.

Pauline, Lincoln's mother, had been raised a Tafoya. She learned pottery making from her mother and grandmother. After marrying Simon, she continued her craft, earning a reputation for making some of the finest black pottery in the pueblo. Her daughter, Joy, was only eighteen, but had already made a name for herself in the cottage industry.

Mother and daughter produced their work on the dining room table. A single pot may take a week to make and another four days to dry. When as many as twenty-four pots had been complete—some decorated—a metal grate was placed on empty tin cans. The pots were carefully arranged on the grate.

Kindling and cow chips were arranged around the base, then metal scrap, such as old cafeteria serving trays, was used to cover the pots, creating a kind of kiln. The fire was lit, and the pottery baked in the makeshift oven. This produced red pottery.

For black pottery, one more step was needed. Dried horse manure was poured over the top of the kiln, smothering the fire underneath. This step prevented the clay from oxidizing and turning red. The manure smoke permeated the pottery, turning it black.

This kind of firing, and the type of clay being used, produced shiny pottery without the need for glaze. The entire firing process could take up to eight hours.

Both Simon and Lincoln were happy to help. This was a family business and some pots sold for hundreds, even thousands of dollars. Simon's regular job was with the Pueblo roads department. His fellow workers understood when he needed to take a day off to fire a kiln.

"I don't want you to do too much," Simon said. "Your mother and Joy both said they would help."

"I'll do what I can."

"Good."

Lincoln toyed with the idea of telling his father what he had seen on Cerro Grande. Maybe later, after the horse manure was dumped over the fire and there was a lull in the action, he would say something.

Chapter Five

Ray Cabrera turned off Highway 296 onto the gravel road that led to the ranch house. He passed a sign that read *Rancho Cazador—The Sportsman's Haven—Professional Guides*. Fresh paint would have done wonders for the faded letters.

It had been a dry winter followed by a drier spring. Cabrera's truck stirred up dust, leaving a haze in the air not unlike the smoke hanging over the buildings of Segovia.

He took a swig from the half-pint of whiskey. Almost empty, he had just bought it that morning . . . after leaving the bank.

"Bastards," he said for the hundredth time, under his breath.

***

"Come on, Robert," Cabrera begged. "I've been dealing with Segovia Savings and Loan for twenty years."

Robert Paredes continued to frown as he nodded. "Ray, I know exactly how long we've had to deal with you . . . not to mention how much you owe."

"Yeah, well, all I'm asking is for you to roll both mortgages into one loan . . ."

"Plus, what did you say? Another ten thousand for operating costs."

Cabrera shrugged. "Since we're doing the paperwork, why don't we make it fifteen thousand? I have to be able to operate until the Fall hunting season."

Paredes turned and typed on his keyboard, then studied the computer screen.

"You're paying twenty-five hundred a month on those two loans. Between now and October you would pay us ten thousand dollars. That alone will eat up any loan we give you."

"So, what am I supposed to do?"

"Tell you what," the loan officer said as he typed something on his screen. "The bank will suspend your payments until the first of October. That's the same thing as a ten-thousand-dollar loan. We'll let the interest accumulate for the next four months."

"You don't seem to understand. I need cash!"

"No, Ray. You don't understand. You owe us over half a million dollars. You're not going to see another red cent from us. I made you an offer. Take it or leave it."

He had no choice but to accept the terms.

***

Cabrera brought the Ram truck to a stop in front of the *Rancho* house and offices. He finished the whiskey and stuffed the bottle under his seat. He knew he wasn't fooling anyone. Especially, not Bess, his wife. She would be able to smell his breath as soon as he walked through the front door. He told others there had to be beagle blood in her family somewhere.

They still played their game. She would accuse him of drinking and driving. He would deny it. Then they both would sulk. Things hadn't changed in thirty years.

"What did the bank say?" Bess asked, walking out of the kitchen while she dried her hands.

"We'll have enough money to get us through the summer."

She stopped ten feet short of her husband. Her expression said, "You've been drinking!"

"Just a half pint," he mumbled, hanging his hat on a peg along the wall.

"So, you got the loan?"

"In a roundabout way."

"What does that mean?"

"That means you shouldn't worry," Cabrera snapped. "I handle the finances."

"Hmph," she said, turning back to the kitchen. "The Andersons called right after you left."

"What? They wanted to complain again about not bagging an Elk. Our brochure says we don't guarantee success."

"No," she said, stopping in the doorway. "They cancelled their slots for the Fall hunt. They want their deposit back."

Cabrera turned white as the blood drained from his face. "Their deposit!" he choked. "They're not going to hunt in October?"

"I think they're still hunting . . . just not with us."

"Not Red Ranch Outfitters!"

"Probably."

Five years earlier, his three best hunting guides, one of which was their twenty-year-old son, walked out, accusing him of cheating them out of their fees. They started Red Ranch Outfitters just ten miles west of his operations. They not only left with their regular clients, they negotiated better terms with the local ranchers, cutting him out of the best hunting ranges.

He blamed his misfortunes on their disloyalty. It never dawned on him it was his fault they had abandoned him. Ray Cabrera would never accept the fact that *Rancho Cazador* was failing because he was a bad businessman and, for the most part, a miserable excuse for a human being.

"I'll call them back," Cabrera said, heading for his office. "I know I can convince them to stay with us."

"Sure, you can."

There was a weariness in Bess' voice. She never exactly forgave him for driving Albert away. After a time, though, her anger softened to acceptance . . . just like everything else in their relationship.

Bess only stayed married to him for one reason . . . pity. She knew he would never survive without her.

Chapter Six

Cañada Creek flowed north from the rim of Valles Caldera for over twenty miles. Its spring-fed waters emptied into Artiga Reservoir, not far from O'Keefe Ranch. Farmers and herders had capitalized on the rich volcanic soil of the Cañada Valley for hundreds of years. The narrow fields of farmland extended from Highway 296 to the Gonzales farm, five miles to the south.

The Gonzales family had operated their stretch of Cañada Creek for over a hundred years. Called an inholding, it was private property long before the Santa Fe National Forest was established around them. At an elevation of 7,200 feet, Esteban Gonzales' choice of crops were limited, but with poultry, sheep and a few cows, his operation was self-sufficient.

Along with five other farmers, he was part of an informal co-op. They pooled their resources to harvest their limited products and deliver them to the Segovia and Santa Fe markets.

Esteban's oldest son would graduate from Segovia High School in a week. Of his five children, the farmer hoped Eric would be the one to stay and work the farm. There were not enough opportunities for all his children to remain in the valley. They would drift away and end up in Las Palmas or Segovia. Maybe even Santa Fe. He hoped they would be close. He loved being a father and looked forward to being a grandfather.

As he stood on his front porch, Esteban looked south. The Jemez Mountains rose sharply from the valley to over 8,500 feet. They blocked his view of the smoke from the Cerro Grande Fire. The news that morning said it was still not under control. He was sure he had nothing to worry about. Cerro Grande was twenty miles south and the wind was blowing the fire to the east.

As he turned to go inside for another cup of coffee, his youngest daughter came running up. She had to occupy herself while the other kids were at school. Edith was out of breath when she said, "Papa, Papa, some of the chickens are gone."

"What do you mean?"

"There are supposed to be twelve chickens and there's only ten."

Gonzalez was surprised at the announcement. Not that there were missing chickens but that his four-year-old knew how to count. "Edie, are you sure?"

"Uh huh." She grabbed one of his thick fingers and pulled. "Come see."

She dragged him across the yard to the chicken coop. The outside chicken run was eight feet by sixteen feet, enclosed with wire mesh, open on the top. The chicken house itself was at one end with an exterior door for easy access to the eggs.

The rooster and seven chickens were milling around the pen, scrounging for food.

"I count eight," Esteban said. "There must be four in the coop."

"I don't think so," Edie said with authority.

Esteban opened the door. Two chickens rested in two of the straw filled nests.

The farmer went back outside and counted the flock again. The total number of chickens was still ten. His first thought was he had been raided by coyotes, though he wasn't sure how they got over the six-foot high wire mesh. He ruled out hawks and racoons. The rooster had defended his flock from hawks before and racoons were too lazy to attack a full-grown chicken.

"Sweet mother of God, Edith, you're right."

"I know."

Gonzales shook his head. Edie sounded more like his wife every day.

"What are we going to do?"

He looked down at his daughter. "What you mean?"

"Are we getting more chickens?"

"Maybe." He wasn't sure that was a good idea. There really was such a thing as a pecking order. If a new chicken was introduced, it might not survive. Other chickens had been known to peck new arrivals to death as they established their dominance.

"I need to cover the top with chicken wire, so we don't lose any more."

He picked up his daughter and headed back to the house.

"Was it a bear?"

"Was what a bear?"

"Did a bear take the chickens?"

Bears emerged from hibernation in April. They were hungry and ill tempered. If a starving bear did climb into the enclosure, Gonzales didn't think it would have been satisfied with just two birds. Besides, they would have eaten them on the spot and the farmer saw no sign of carnage.

"I don't think so. A bear wouldn't take them away. He would have eaten them in the pen. There would have been feathers everywhere."

"A mama bear could take them if her cubs wanted to eat."

The farmer stopped and looked at the child he carried. He never paid much attention to their conversations. She was just a baby. "How did you get so smart?"

"I don't know," Edie shrugged. "I just am."

Chapter Seven

"Jimmy didn't come home last night," Ramona Clay complained. "Where is he?"

"I-I don't know," Tito stammered into the phone. It was the second lie he had told that morning . . . maybe third. He pushed the office door closed to muffle the sound of pneumatic tools. The four bays of *Luis' Car Repair and Body Shop* were full. More cars were parked in the lot awaiting attention.

"You two went out together! You always go out together!"

"Well, not-not together. We met up at *Ohkay Casino*. Had a couple beers. Played some slots. I had to leave early."

"What time was that?"

"I don't know. Eight, eight thirty. I had to drive up to Dixon, help *Tia* Gloria with her plumbing."

Tia Gloria didn't have a phone. Tito hoped his sister didn't push the issue. He hadn't come up with an explanation of how he knew their aunt needed help.

"That *pendejo* got drunk," Ramona said, bitterly. "I just know it."

"Maybe. Cops might have picked him up. He could be in jail," Tito suggested.

"Yeah, probably. At least he didn't come home and beat me again. Did Luis say anything when Jimmy didn't show up to work?"

"Not much," Calle lied again.

"This will be the third time this month he missed work." Ramona sounded like she was crying. "He's going to lose his job! We can't live just on what I make."

Tito's heart was breaking. He hated to hear his little sister cry. He didn't have the *cajones* to tell her Jimmy had been fired already.

***

Tito Calle now regretted ever meeting Jimmy Clay. They first joined up in high school. Jimmy was a natural leader and Tito needed someone to follow.

Clay was a schemer . . . always had big ideas. They were mostly ways to make money, a lot of which were illegal. Petty theft ranked high on his list of preferred larceny. Tito went along, mostly because he wasn't bright enough to think for himself.

The two stole a car once, just before graduation. It wasn't for a joy ride or a thrill. Jimmy had already arranged to deliver the car to a chop-shop outside Santa Fe. It was a quick two hundred dollars. The two teenagers watched the operation for an hour. They were amazed how quickly the Chevy was dismantled into individual parts. They were surprised to find out the car parts were worth far more individually than when assembled.

Jimmy Clay knew what direction he wanted his life to take. He wanted one day to operate his own auto chop-shop. He needed to know about cars though. He and Tito both took classes at Northern New Mexico College to become automobile mechanics. When they got their certificates, they were hired by Luis Ramis to work at his repair shop.

Jimmy's goal all along had been to open a repair shop that could be a front for stolen cars. Something like that took money. His job didn't pay nearly enough. In a short time, he was back to stealing again, dragging Tito Calle along with him.

Jimmy Clay had always been a bully, though. Something Tito overlooked, just so he could be close to his "mentor." Tito was actually thrilled when Jimmy showed interest in his sister, two years his junior. He thought the marriage would be a perfect fit for his friendship with Clay.

On top of being a bully, Jimmy Clay was a drunk . . . a mean drunk at that. He had pushed Tito around many a time. Calle thought nothing of it . . . just a price to pay to be around his leader. He never realized his sister, Ramona, suffered beatings from her husband on a regular basis . . . her and her five-year-old son. The beatings were worse when Jimmy came home drunk, a situation that happened more and more often.

Ramona was short and plump and didn't think another man would have her. That's what Jimmy always told her, so she suffered in silence.

It was Linda, Tito's wife, who finally alerted him to Ramona's situation a month earlier.

Tito didn't want to believe it. Jimmy and Ramona had been married for six years. If it was that bad, why hadn't she left already. He finally understood how bad Ramona was treated when she came to his house, and he saw for himself.

Calle tried to broach the subject with Clay, but Jimmy shut him down each time. It was none of his business. Tito needed to shut up and do what he was told.

The result was Tito's anger only festered. It exploded the night before, after the two loaded three sets of mag wheels into the stolen van. Calle worked up the courage to actually confront Clay about his sister.

Jimmy slapped him hard, nearly knocking him to the ground, just to remind him who was in charge. The Buck knife on Tito's belt had a four-inch blade. Before Calle realized it, the knife was in his hand, and he was plunging it again and again into Jimmy's chest.

It was too dark for Tito to see the shocked expression on Jimmy's face. It was the first time in over ten years that Calle stood up to him. It would also be the last.

***

"Don't cry, little sister," Tito begged. "I'm sure Jimmy will show up."

"Should I call the police?

"No, no, I wouldn't do that."

"What if he comes home drunk again?"

"Grab little Jimmy and go to my place. You know where we hide the key. Just wait in our trailer till me or Linda get home."

The office door flew open.

"Calle, are you still on that phone?" Luis Ramis stormed. "We've got cars backing up. You want to end up like your worthless brother-in-law?"

"Ramona, I gotta go. We'll talk this evening."

Chapter Eight

Tina Morales had moved to Lansing's ranch the previous September to recuperate from major surgery. She was supposed to convalesce for six weeks. Despite her doctor's protests, she insisted that she had to get back to work. All she needed from him was a signed release.

Tina was teaching again before the end of October.

The two of them flew to Phoenix for Thanksgiving. One of the sheriff's rare vacations. He was sorry he couldn't join her again at Christmas. He needed to stay in Las Palmas so his deputies could have time with their families.

Since the first of the year, they had fallen into a comfortable routine. Tina did most of the cooking, though they always went out to eat on Wednesday evening. Tourist season hadn't started yet, so that night Lansing suggested the *High Desert Restaurant* in Cohino.

"One of my students asked why we haven't been going to church," the chemistry teacher said, taking a sip of wine.

"Did you say we got tired of Father Roberto scowling at us for living in sin?"

Tina shrugged. "I guess I should have. I always remember what my grandmother said about the Pope and contraceptives. 'If he no play the game; he no make the rules.'

"I feel the same way about our sinful ways. Besides, in the church's eyes a woman's greatest contribution to a family is children. Since I can't have kids now, I have nothing to contribute."

Lansing couldn't help but notice her bitterness. He knew it wouldn't help to point it out. That would start an argument. He also suspected her anger was with the church and not her recent medical issues. He thought she had handled her condition with grace and dignity.

He had his own view about the Catholic church. He was divorced. The church refused to recognize divorce. According to the rules he could not get remarried. To do so would be a sin. Living with Tina was a sin. He was allegedly damned in the sight of God, no matter what he did. He understood why people shopped for churches.

"It sounds like they got the people out of Los Alamos just in time," he said, changing the subject. "As of about five this evening, they had lost two dozen homes."

"That's terrible." She sounded like she appreciated the diversion. "Has anyone been killed?"

"No, not that I've heard."

"Thank God for that . . . How large is the town?"

"Somewhere around eighteen thousand. Everything there is geared to support the Los Alamos Labs in one way or another. It's been that way for over fifty years."

"Do they still make atomic bombs there?"

"I don't know. I'm sure they still do atomic research. Why?"

"I'm worried about what happens if the fire reaches the laboratories. One of my students asked if they thought there could be a nuclear explosion."

"What did you tell them?"

"No, of course not. Nuclear bombs aren't like regular explosives. Even a fire won't set them off. But that doesn't mean nuclear contamination couldn't be released if their containers were breached."

Lansing knitted his brows. "That's a possibility?"

"That's always a possibility. The Manhattan Project let the genie out of the bottle and there's no putting it back."

"Well," Lansing sputtered, "I'm sure the government is prepared for all contingencies."

"Yes, just like they were ready for Three Mile Island . . . or how the Russians were prepared for Chernobyl?"

"This certainly turned into an appetizing conversation."

"It's your fault. You're the one who brought up the fire."

"I did do that, didn't I?"

"You did."

He held up his empty beer bottle. When he caught the waitress' eye, he tapped it.

"Would you like some more wine?"

"Why not? I don't have to grade papers again until August."

Chapter Nine

After dinner, Pauline and Joy sat at the dining room table studying a broken bowl. Of the twenty-four pieces fired that afternoon, twenty-three came out perfectly. One of Joy's bowls "exploded." It wasn't a major explosion. No other pieces were damaged. But the bowl with the grey on black hummingbird motif had shattered into a dozen pieces.

"It looks like the imperfection was at the center of the plate," Pauline observed. "See how the breaks radiate from the middle."

Joy shook her head. She had only eight pieces in the kiln. A senior at Segovia High School, she would graduate in a week. Once she finished with school, her plan was to craft pottery full time. "That wasn't the last piece I finished. It had plenty of time to dry out before we fired it."

Her mother shrugged. "I know you're frustrated. The only other thing I can suggest is you left an air bubble in the clay. The bubble expanded from the heat, fracturing the brittle clay around it."

Lincoln half listened to the women discuss their craftwork. He marveled at how calmly and analytical they were over a broken piece of pottery.

There was a part of him that envied his sister. Joy had a talent he could never hope to embrace. She started handling pottery clay when she was eight. Her mother wouldn't let her "play" with it. The clay was sacred and had to be treated with respect.

Pauline explained that the malleable piece of the earth had to be talked to and prayed over. The potter influenced the clay in a spiritual way, just as the clay, in turn, influenced the potter. Such an attitude was typical among the Tewa Pueblos. The Tewa Cosmos was a spiritual Cosmos that permeated the whole society . . . in theory, anyway.

***

Of the seven Tewa speaking pueblos, San Juan Pueblo north of Segovia and its *Ohkay Owingeh* people adhered closest to the historical concept of a Summer and Winter moiety or clan. The Spanish established a secular structure to pueblo governance in the 17th Century. The governor, lieutenant governor, sheriff and church officials were selected annually by the chiefs of the moieties.

At the dawn of the 21st Century, this centuries-old system operated, in one way or another, in every pueblo except Santa Clara. A schism in the 1890s between the two moieties nearly destroyed the pueblo.

The split was driven by dominant personalities in both clans and the result affected all political and religious activities. For nearly forty years, Winter members refused to participate in Summer Society religious dances, and vice versa. This affected community obligations such as preparing the fields for irrigation or fixing roads. The Summer Moiety, through various means, managed to control the secular government until 1935.

In that year the federal government introduced the Indian Reorganization Act. The legislation was designed to encourage the Indian Nations to accept constitutional forms of government. Santa Clara was the only pueblo to seize the opportunity. By moving to a democratic system, the positions of Governor, Lieutenant Governor, and Sheriff were elected by popular vote. Since the moieties no longer had the means to control the secular power in the Pueblo, they reverted to purely religious organizations.

***

Lincoln's attention was immediately drawn to the ringing phone in the kitchen.

"I'll get it," Simon Baca said, getting up from the sofa.

Lincoln looked at the time. Nine o'clock seemed a little late for a call, unless it was one of Joy's friends. When his sister got started, she might talk until the early hours of the morning.

Pauline insisted Joy use some of her pottery money to purchase a cell phone. The rest of the family needed access to the outside world, too.

When Simon didn't gesture for Joy to come to the phone, the firefighter knew something serious was happening.

He strained to hear his father. All he could pick up was an occasional "uh-huh, uh-huh," "I see," or "Sure, sure."

Simon ended the conversation with, "Don't worry. I'll be there."

He noticed his family staring at him as he hung up the phone.

"Is it the fire?" Pauline asked.

He simply nodded.

"Is it bad?" Lincoln tried to hide his self-disappointment.

"It's getting that way. The Forest Service asked us to position our heavy equipment beyond the Puye Cliffs. We may have to make some fire breaks in the Santa Fe Forest to keep it away from the Pueblo."

"Where's the fire now?" It was Joy's turn.

"It's in Los Alamos. Also, at the National Labs. They've already sent city fire crews from Segovia and Santa Fe to help."

Simon understood his family's concerns. He felt the same way.

"I don't think we have anything to worry about," he lied. "I'm going to bed. I have to get up early."

Chapter Ten

Lincoln stared at the ceiling in the darkness. He was forced to sleep on his back, something he wasn't used to. The cast strapped against his stomach was cumbersome in the day and uncomfortable at night.

His eagerness to help his father with the kiln earlier in the day was short lived. The doctors had told him to rest and let his bones mend.

"What the hell do they know?" he thought to himself. "That kind of advice was for little kids or old men." He was twenty-one and in great health. He would show them. He would heal twice as fast as the doctors forecast.

After situating the iron grate on the tin cans to allow the heat to be distributed evenly, the two men began arranging the pottery. Bending over to pick up the individual items, then stretching across the grate to place them face down, was a bigger strain on Lincoln than he anticipated. With only one hand to work with, his movements were clumsy, and he almost dropped three of the bowls.

He had to get on his knees to position the dried cedar wood for the fire. This, too, was more of a strain than he anticipated. Halfway through positioning the scrap metal over the pottery, Lincoln had to quit.

He hurt . . . He also discovered pain wore you out.

Going inside, he fell asleep on the sofa and stayed there for most of the afternoon.

Joy replaced him at the kiln.

The firefighter guessed he couldn't sleep because of his time on the couch. But something else was bothering him as well.

At first, he thought it was anger. He certainly was angry with himself over tripping and falling. The broken bones were caused by his own negligence.

Something else, though, was eating away at him. He felt left out, like the world was passing him by. Any armchair psychologist could have told him he was depressed, but it was a feeling foreign to him. He didn't know that simply talking to another person was the easiest path to recovery.

He had missed the opportunity to talk with his father. He had to abandon their project because of his pain, so he missed out on the slack time while the pots were fired. He wanted to discuss what he had seen on Cerro Grande. After a week in the haze of pain killers, he began to have doubts. He needed reassurance that what he had seen was real.

He also wondered . . . did the creatures escape the fire? Did they blame him and the other firefighters for the destruction of their forest?

Shouldering that idea as his own responsibility sunk him deeper into his depression.

Chapter Eleven

Jack Rivera gave a short rap on the door jam.

"You wanted to see me, Cliff?"

"I did, Jack. Where are we on the Western Auto break-in?"

The Chief Deputy stepped into the office and sat in the chair in front of his boss' desk.

"Frankly, nowhere. I put Jake Redwine on telephone duty yesterday. He called every hospital and clinic within a hundred and fifty miles. No one was treated for gunshot or stab wounds. No dead bodies reported anywhere.

"I talked to Harry Avila again. Tried to get an idea about the size of truck needed to haul off those rims. He guessed it would take something a bit bigger than a pickup. Possibly a cargo van."

"Or two pickup trucks," the sheriff added. "I don't think these thieves will pawn them. Wouldn't make enough money. I'm thinking they'll try to sell them on the internet."

"Sure, like eBay," Rivera agreed. "I have Danny Cortez on office shift today. I'll have him start looking on the web."

"Good." Lansing held up a sheet of paper.

"What's that?"

"The county Democrats want to know if I'm running for reelection."

"You are, aren't you?"

"Tina asked me the same thing last night."

"What did you tell her?"

"I told her I like my job . . . I just hate the politics. I doubly hate campaigning."

"You're what . . . forty-four?"

"I will be, this year."

"So, you're going to run for a third term. What's the problem?"

"Nothing, really."

"Has anyone said they'll run against you?"

"I heard a rumor that the Segovia Police Chief might."

"Ernie Solano? Are you sure?"

"I'm sure it's a rumor if that's what you mean."

"He's from Segovia, isn't he?"

"Yeah."

"Why would he want to move to Las Palmas?"

"Maybe he's tired of being confined to one town. He might be ready to tackle bigger territory."

"Instead of guessing, why don't you ask him outright?"

The sheriff smiled. "I'm waiting for him to call me back." He knitted his brows. "You're not interested, are you?"

"For Sheriff? You must be nuts. I would shoot at least one of the County Commissioners after the first budget meeting. Maybe all three.

"I like being Under Sheriff just fine. I don't mind stepping in when you're out of pocket. But full time?" Rivera stood. "Forget it."

"Just checking, Jack. Just checking."

As Rivera left, Lansing's phone rang.

"This is Lansing."

"Yeah, Boss," Clem Montoya said. "We got a list of road closures from the State Police."

"I'll come up front."

After filling his coffee mug, Lansing retrieved the list from his Desk Sergeant. Standing in front of the wall map, he mentally marked the restricted roads.

State Highway 30 was closed south of Santa Clara Pueblo. State Road 4 through Bandelier National Monument was shut down completely. State Highway 504 was blocked to westbound traffic starting at San Ildefonso Pueblo.

Highway 15, the north-south main road for the county, was still open.

"Where's the fire now?"

Marylin Bea looked up from her position at dispatch.

"They said on the radio fire crews are holding their own in Los Alamos, but the winds have spread the fire south of town. They started evacuating White Rock after midnight."

"Damn!" Lansing swore. He turned to Montoya. "Clemente, contact the State Police. Ask if there's anything our office can do to help."

"Sure thing, Sheriff."

Los Alamos County was suffering the brunt of the Cerro Grande Fire as it was now designated. The small town of White Rock sat at the Santa Fe County line.

City Fire Departments from Segovia and Santa Fe were being reinforced by units from Albuquerque and Farmington to combat the structure fires in Los Alamos. The U.S. Forestry Service, the Park Service and the New Mexico Forestry Departments were all involved now.

The Santa Clara Pueblo Reservation stretched for twenty miles from the Rio Grande west to the Jemez Mountains. The eastern half of the reservation was in San Phillipe County, the western half in Sandoval.

Barely four miles from Los Alamos, Lansing knew how easily the fire could spread to the Santa Clara Reservation. With few roads in the Santa Fe National Forest, it would be near impossible for fire crews to intercept the flames as they pushed north.

The sheriff reconsidered his commitment to avoid the church. Now might be a good time to light a candle, maybe say a prayer for the hundreds of men and women fighting the fire.

Chapter Twelve

Ray Cabrera poked at his *huevos rancheros*. He was more sullen than usual.

"What's wrong?" Bess knew what his problem was. She hoped getting him to talk about it might relieve the pressure.

"Nothing's wrong," he growled.

"You're not eating."

"I'm not hungry." He pushed away the plate of eggs and beans. Standing, he retrieved his hat from the wall peg and headed for the door.

"Where are you going?"

"Lobo Creek Store. I need to gas up my truck."

"Didn't you gas up yesterday?"

"No . . . Not since I left the bank."

Bess only half believed him. She had seen his foul moods before. They usually proceeded a drinking bout that could last for days. Being the only general mercantile store for miles around, *Lobo Creek Market* sold everything, including whiskey.

"Are you coming right back?"

"No. I need to talk to a couple of ranchers about hunting leases."

"So, you'll be home for lunch?"

"Maybe. I don't know."

He was out the door without saying goodbye or giving his wife a parting kiss . . . something she was getting used to.

Bess cleared the dining room table. After scraping the leftovers into their dog's bowl, she busied herself with dishes, then general housework. She tried not to think about her husband or their mounting financial problems.

Periodically, she would stop and stare at the phone. She wanted to make the call. If Ray ever found out, he would slap her around more than just a little. It had happened before.

After an hour, she quit debating with herself and picked up the receiver. She dialed in the number and waited.

"Red Ranch Outfitters, Ben Gallegos speaking."

"Hello, Benjamin. This is Bess Cabrera. Is my son available?"

"Yes, ma'am . . . Just a minute."

In the background, she could hear Gallegos yell, "Al . . . phone call!"

A moment later another voice said, "This is Albert."

"Hi, son . . ."

"Oh, hi, Mama. This is a pleasant surprise."

"I was wondering, Albert, if you had time to talk."

Albert was quiet for a moment. "I know what you want to talk about, Mama. The Andersons out of Tulsa. When we took their reservation, I didn't know they cancelled with dad. They didn't say anything until the very end.

"We're not hurting for bookings. If you want us to cancel them, I'll see what I can do. Of course, I need to clear it with John and Ben."

"No, no. Please, don't. That's not why I called."

"Is something wrong?"

"I'll be honest. It looks like *Rancho Cazador* isn't going to make it to hunting season this year."

"Oh, Mama. I'm so sorry! Listen, I'll cancel the Andersons immediately."

"I don't want you to do that! One booking for the Fall hunt won't save us."

"You know I will do anything to help. What do you want me to do?"

"I've accepted that we'll lose the ranch. We'll start over again. We've done it before."

"Not when you were in your fifties, though." He paused. "You didn't call me up to tell me you are going to lose the ranch. What do you need, Mama?"

It was Bess' turn to pause. "Your father started drinking again."

"Come on, Mom. He never quit!"

"I know . . . I'm just afraid he'll drink himself to death, this time."

Albert wanted to ask if that was necessarily a bad thing. Instead, he asked, "What do you want me to do?"

"He needs something to keep him occupied. He needs to get his mind off the ranch. If he's not worried about finances, maybe he won't drink so much."

"I refuse to hire him! He wouldn't take an order from me anyway."

"I don't want you to hire him. I know in the off-season you boys drive sheep and cattle to the high pastures for some of the ranchers. If a job like that comes along, maybe you could refer your father. If he's working, maybe he won't be drinking."

"It never stopped him before," Albert said under his breath. Then, louder, he responded, "I'll see what I can do, Mom."

"Thanks, Albert. I love you!"

"Love you, too, Mama!"

Chapter Thirteen

"Esteban, you need some help there?"

Gonzales recognized the voice as he looked over his shoulder. "Hey, Vern. As a matter of fact . . ." He stopped fighting with the chicken wire and climbed down from his ladder. ". . . I was almost ready to have my wife come out and help."

"Putting a top on your chicken run?" Vernon Sanchez asked. Sanchez lived a half mile down the road and was Esteban's closest neighbor.

"Yeah. Lost two chickens, night before last. I think it was a bear."

"Really? How do you know?"

"Come around on this side." Gonzales led his fellow farmer to the opposite side of the enclosure. He pointed to where the wire had been stretched, by paws presumably. The culprit used the wire fence to boost himself into the run. "Looks like he climbed right over the top."

Vernon nodded. "You're not the only one with problems. I lost a lamb last night. Something grabbed it out of the pasture. Found a couple of tracks. Must have been from a bear. Those tracks were big.

"I was getting ready to move the flock to the top of the mesa. That won't happen till we take care of this problem."

"What? Trap it and move it somewhere else?"

"That's what the Fish and Wildlife rangers do. But they've got their hands full with that damned fire south of here."

As Vernon finished his sentence, the "whap-whap-whapping" of large rotor blades could be heard. They looked up to see a red helicopter heading north. Fifty feet below it hung an orange-colored, Bambi Bucket for transporting water.

"Heading up to Artiga Reservoir," Esteban observed. "That's the closest place they can scoop up water. Bet they're making twenty trips a day. How much water do those things hold?"

"I heard some can carry over two thousand gallons. For that, though, they got to use a big military helicopter . . . I think they're called Chinooks. That red one that just went over probably grabs a thousand gallons a scoop."

Esteban nodded. "You'd think they could put out a fire with all that water." He returned to the problem at hand. "If Fish and Wildlife can't help us with that bear, what are we supposed to do?"

"Kill it."

"It's not bear season till late summer."

"Doesn't matter. We can shoot those *maldito ladrones* (damned thieves) any time they're a nuisance. In season or not."

Esteban let out a deep sigh. "I suppose we get to sit up all night to guard our property."

"Hell, that's what I got a son for. Adam can sit next to the pasture with a gun just as well as I can."

"Eric can, too," Gonzales admitted. "But tomorrow's Friday. They still have school."

"The boys graduate next week," Vern said. "From what I hear, all their tests are over and done with. If they miss a day, *lo que*? So what?"

"I guess you're right."

Esteban walked back to his ladder. Picking up the chicken wire, he said, "If you can help hold this in place, I have a staple gun."

Vern stepped closer to secure the wire. "Is this new fencing?"

"Yeah. Picked it up in Segovia yesterday."

"Could you see the smoke from the fire?"

"It was everywhere. The wind's blowing right over the town."

"I've heard both Los Alamos and White Rock were cleared out."

"Well, they'd better do something or they're going to lose Segovia, too. If you draw a straight line, Segovia and Los Alamos can't be more than eight miles apart."

"I don't know. That's a lot of territory for a fire to eat up."

Gonzales began stapling the chicken wire into place. After securing a four-foot stretch of wire mesh, he stepped down to move his ladder. "All I can say is 'Thank God' that fire's nowhere close to us. It's somebody else's problem."

Chapter Fourteen

"I am flattered you think I'm a potential rival, Cliff," Ernesto Solano laughed over the phone. His was a deep, resonate sound erupting from his ample belly. "I couldn't run for an office in San Phillipe County even if I wanted . . . not unless I moved."

"What do you mean?"

"I live about two blocks outside the county line. I'm in Santa Fe County."

Solano's laugh was infectious. Lansing joined in, mostly because he was relieved that he faced no competition for reelection. "I didn't know that, Ernie."

"Segovia's location is so damned convoluted you don't know if you're coming or going."

"I know what you mean." Half of the town was in San Phillipe, the other half in Santa Fe. "I'm never quite sure when I'm out of my own jurisdiction."

"It's not only that. Part of town is on the Santa Clara Pueblo grant. We have to pay for right of way on our own city streets."

"I forget about that." Lansing let his laugh fade. "Listen, Ernie, I wanted to ask how bad things are getting with that fire down your way?"

"We're safe for now, but our firefighting resources are getting spread thin. Most of our trucks have been sent to Los Alamos. I heard a few hearty souls even refused to leave their homes. A lot of the evacuees went to White Rock. They had to move again early this morning."

"We're getting some. Most are heading for Santa Fe . . . Oops. I need to get off, Cliff. I got another call coming in."

"Sure, Chief. Talk to you later."

Lansing had avoided the southern part of the county on purpose. With evacuees, firefighting personnel, and emergency vehicles clogging roads, local and state police didn't need outside observers getting in their way. On the other hand, he was the chief elected law enforcement officer in the county. Didn't he have an obligation to see for himself what was happening?

He grabbed his Stetson and headed for the front office.

"Clem, I'm going out for a while. I'll be on the radio."

"Okay, Boss."

By road it was sixty-six miles from Las Palmas to Segovia . . . another twenty to Los Alamos. Lansing guessed the fire was sixty miles due south of the county seat. Highway 15 paralleled Rio Cohino. It snaked its way between hills, heading both east and west, but generally south.

The sheriff kept glancing from the road to the sky over Los Alamos, wondering when the smoke clouds would appear. It wasn't until he crested a hill after the passing Artiga Reservoir that the billowing clouds began to appear.

The fire was thirty miles away. Mesas and mountain peaks, some over ten thousand feet, no longer blocked the view. He couldn't tell how high the smoke went, five, maybe ten thousand feet above the highest terrain.

When he was ten miles closer, he could see the clouds churning and growing. As he passed the northern Segovia city limits, he slowed and turned onto the access road for the State Police—District 7 Headquarters.

"Dispatch, Patrol One. I'll be out of my unit. You can reach me on my cell."

"Dispatch copies, Sheriff," Marilyn responded.

Lansing got out of his Jeep and looked to the southwest. The center of Los Alamos was ten miles away. The wall of billowing smoke extended for ten miles, north/south. The wind, now blowing fifty-miles-an-hour, was pushing the smoke towards him. He couldn't see flames from his position. He could only guess how frightening the sight must be at night.

***

"The operation seems disjointed to me," Captain David Ortiz said, waving his hand over the topographic map spread over a conference table. "The Incident Command Post was set up at the Los Alamos Labs headquarters. They're trying to save as many structures as they can and protect any hazardous material.

"The National Park Service is trying to protect Bandelier. They've managed to keep the fire north of State Highway four, but I think that's because the wind has been on their side."

He pointed to the canyons north of Los Alamos. "The Forest Service is coordinating the efforts to the east and north."

"What about the forests to the west?" Lansing asked.

"I'm sure they have crews out there, but Baca Ranch is still private property. The prevailing winds are from the south and west, so, Valles Caldera looks safe."

"Where's the fire now?"

Ortiz traced his finger from Cerro Grande Peak eastward. "The fire jumped Highway 501, about three-quarters of a mile past their fire line. It's moving so fast they can barely keep up. That's why they evacuated White Rock.

"They had been flying air operations out of Albuquerque, but those got suspended because of the high winds."

"What about to the north?"

"As of yesterday, the fire was two miles outside of Los Alamos. If it gets across Guaje Canyon," the captain pointed to a deep, east/west arroyo a mile north of Los Alamos, "there's nothing to keep it from reaching the Santa Clara Reservation."

"How many firefighting personnel are working the blazes?"

"Last count I heard about five hundred and seventy with more on the way. That doesn't count the support personnel. When they fought the Dome Fire, they built a tent city overnight, with catering, sleeping tents, even mobile hospitals."

Lansing whistled. "Casualties?"

"I'm sure there are injuries, but I haven't heard of a single loss of human life."

"Thank God for that," the sheriff nodded.

"Yeah," Ortiz agreed.

"How much help do you need from me and my deputies, David?"

"None, Sheriff. I have patrol people from all over the state at my disposal. We're just trying to keep civilians out of danger and stay out of the way. Let the professionals do their jobs."

Chapter Fifteen

Pauline Baca was tired of her son moping around the house. "Why don't you do something useful?"

"Dammit, Mama," Lincoln blurted. "I can't!"

"Unless you want a slap . . ." She raised her hand in a threat. ". . . don't you dare swear at me."

"Sorry. I'm sorry, Mama. Really," he quickly apologized. "It's just that . . . I don't know what I can do. I was worse than useless yesterday around the kiln."

His mother understood what he meant. Simon had to restack almost every pot his son tried to position on the grate. It would have taken her husband half as much time if he had done the work alone.

"So, what's wrong with your legs?"

"Nothing." He gave his mother a quizzical look.

"I need to do some cleaning around here. You're just going to be in my way."

"You want me to leave?"

"Yes. I want you to go to the Senior Center. My Uncle Eluterio goes there every day they're open. Go keep him company."

Lincoln almost protested. He had gotten little sleep and was anticipating a restful morning on the sofa. However, one reason for not sleeping was his concern over what he had seen on Cerro Grande. He wanted to talk to his father, but that was an opportunity missed.

His Great-uncle Eluterio, even though he was approaching ninety, was still sharp and a source for endless stories. (As he grew older, Lincoln suspected not every story was true, but they were always entertaining.)

"What time should I come back for lunch?"

"Stay there." Pauline was about to have the house to herself for the first time in a week. "They'll feed you."

It was a ten-minute walk from the Baca house to the Pueblo Senior Center on Kee Street. Lincoln admitted to himself that it felt good to stretch his legs. The outdoors was cool. However, the smoke from the Cerro Grande Fire, looming like a threatening giant, was now settling over the pueblo like a menacing fog.

The ground trembled from heavy traffic. A mile away a steady stream of trucks rumbled down Highway 30 to Route 5, the Puye Cliffs access road. Spike Camps, temporary eating and sleeping spots for fire-fighting crews, were being established to the west and south of the cliffs. These areas eliminated the need to travel to the Base Camp at Los Alamos every night.

However, the crews still needed to be fed and other provisions re-plenished daily, so, supplies were brought in from the Incident Command Post. The firefighters themselves started their day at 7:00 am and worked until 11:00 pm. Lunch and dinner breaks were as short as ten minutes. A fire assignment, called a roll, could last up to fourteen days.

Lincoln thought about the ten men he started with on Cerro Grande a week earlier. He imagined they were still fighting the fire, though, dozens of Indian firefighters had already been added to the force. Even the Taos Snowballs, the BIA Hotshot Crew of firefighting specialists, had deployed.

The atmosphere in the Pueblo was subdued. He passed within a block of the Pueblo's Catholic Church. It was abandoned at the moment.

He crossed the bridge over the Santa Clara Creek. The creek was still carrying Spring snowmelt, though it was little more than a trickle. The stone-lined banks were a hundred feet apart, designed to handle the summer monsoon rains.

Across the street from the Senior Center, the *Kha'p'o* Community School was quiet. The one hundred and twenty students were sequestered inside. No one wanted to venture out to observe the growing menace only ten miles away.

Whatever respite from depression his short walk offered had dissolved by the time Lincoln reached the Senior Center.

Chapter Sixteen

Uncle Eluterio Tafoya sat in a chair staring out an easterly facing window. What should have been a sunny, May morning was shrouded by the ever-present smoke. The sun had already risen above the Sangre de Christo Mountains and now hid behind white and grey clouds . . . clouds being pushed and prodded by gusting winds.

A dozen other elderly men and women sat at tables, some doing puzzles, four played cards, others stared at the floor.

"Good morning, Uncle."

Eluterio turned to look at his grandnephew. "Lincoln! My goodness, boy. I heard you fell."

"I did, Uncle, and I wouldn't recommend it."

Tafoya nodded his head. "Do you have time to sit and talk? That would be good."

"That's why I came." Baca found an empty chair and pulled it closer.

The old man reached out and touched the cast. "Does it hurt?"

"My arm, not so much." He gestured toward his left shoulder. "My collar bone hurts, especially when I lie down."

Eluterio frowned. "You broke that, too?"

"Yeah. I was a mess."

"How did that happen?"

Lincoln couldn't have asked for a better opening. He told his uncle about how the Black Mesa Crew had been drafted to fight a "controlled" fire, how it quickly got out of hand, and his eventual trek down the mountain a second time.

Tafoya listened intently, especially when Lincoln described the creatures he encountered.

"I don't understand why you ran," the old man commented. "You said they had already walked past you."

Baca started to shrug, then realized how painful the gesture would be. Instead, he nodded. "I think I was a little scared . . . but mostly I was in a hurry to tell someone else what I saw."

"What did they say when you told them?"

Baca frowned. "You're the first person I said anything to."

"Why?" Eluterio was surprised.

"I was embarrassed that I had fallen . . . Then I didn't even think about them at all when I was in the hospital. They gave me a lot of pain medications. After a day, I believed I imagined the whole thing."

"But you're telling me now."

"I know. I haven't been sleeping well. I keep thinking about those things on the mountain . . . and the fire our crew started . . . and if they escaped . . . or if they didn't, how it was our fault."

Tafoya turned his gaze to the window. "You did not imagine what you saw."

"You've seen them?"

"When I was much younger. When I still hunted, I saw one once. My grandfather said it was an *atosle* . . . an ogre that could swallow a child whole. But I don't think they are so evil. They are also known as *Towa Yoh*, a bear that walks like a man. They come from the *tsin fo nuneh,* the labyrinths under the mountains."

"Are you sure it wasn't a bear?"

"Bears are brown or black. What I saw was red. But like bears, the hair covered its whole body."

"These *atosle* . . . Are they human?"

"Maybe more like us than like bears. For us, this is an ancient memory. We have known about them, lived peacefully with them since our emergence from the *Sipofene.*

"The *atosle* you met on the mountain knew this. He acknowledged you as a fellow traveler on this earth, wanting nothing more than to be left alone . . . him and his family."

"So, he would have never harmed me?"

"Only if you had done injury to him first . . . or to his mate . . . or children."

Lincoln leaned back in his seat and thought about Uncle Eluterio's words. They were a relief. He didn't imagine his encounter.

"As we are taught from childhood, we did not always live here in *Kha'po Owingeh*. We settled in Singing Water Village not long before the Spanish came . . ."

Lincoln nodded. The Spanish established permanent residence among the Tewa Pueblos in the late 1500s. Before then, the Puye Cliff Dwellings four miles to the west had been their home for over three hundred years. The cliff dwellings and the village ruins on Puye Mesa were a huge tourist attraction and a point of pride. Drought had driven the Santa Clara people to the banks of the Rio Grande to establish their present home. The always flowing river provided the water for their crops.

"But even before Puye . . ." Tafoya continued . . . "the Tewa People wandered for many, many years . . . after we emerged from the underworld, the *Sipofene*, beneath Sandy Place Lake.

"Some say we lived for a time at Mesa Verde. But we came to the south where it was warmer, and we could grow our crops. When our fathers crossed the San Juan River near Colorado, they came upon a village of *atosle*.

"These hairy humans did not know how to farm. They fished and hunted using just their hands. They were so big and fast they could run down a deer.

"Some stories say we traded with them. Others say we met then parted with little contact. It is always said the *atosle* were not handsome creatures. But they did not attack people. Not until the Navajo and Apache moved to the San Juan Valley. The *atosles* scattered. I think they were driven away by the new invaders.

"The *atosles* are still here, though. The Navajo, the Jicarilla Apache, see them often. Sometimes they will come from the mountains and raid our crops. They love very much to eat melons and green corn."

These were stories Lincoln had never heard before. "The sheep and goats? Did they try to take the flocks?"

Eluterio nodded. "Oh, yes . . . but I think not often. Bears, mountain lions, coyotes . . . when they take our lambs they are hunted and killed. The *atosles* know that. They are smart."

"Are there many of them?"

Tafoya allowed himself the hint of a smile. "How many times have you seen them?"

Baca blushed for such a stupid question. "Once."

"Then, no. There are not many. And the ones that do exist know how to blend into the forest so they can't be seen."

Lunch was bean soup with cornbread. Lincoln stayed and visited with his great uncle until the Senior Center closed at 2:00.

Chapter Seventeen

"Ramona's really upset," Linda Calle said.

Tito had just walked in from work. He was tired from missing so much sleep the night before. He was exhausted from racking his brains trying to figure out what to do with the stolen property hidden in the old barn. He was worried about someone finding the dead body and tracing it to him. All he wanted to do now was eat, shower, and sleep.

"About Jimmy?" he asked, trying to sound casual. "He isn't home yet?"

"No," she said sharply. "And your sister is worried something happened to him."

"Why? Jimmy was never good to her."

Linda ignored his observation. "She called the police to see if he was in jail. She even called the hospitals to see if he was hurt somewhere."

"You picked him up last night, didn't you?"

"No, no. We met up at the casino. He was there already. That's the last time I saw him. Remember, I had to leave early to fix Tia Gloria's toilet."

Linda, like Ramona, hadn't questioned how Tito's aunt called him without a phone, not to mention when. Calle was sure that if he stuck to his story, why he was out so late wouldn't be suspicious.

Linda nodded. It seemed her husband was always out in the evenings helping others . . . at least once a week. Sometimes Tito and Jimmy also took on outside work to bring in extra money.

Linda never questioned any surplus cash because Tito always handed it over to her. They had two sons, five and six. Her fulltime job was taking care of them. Any money left over went into savings.

She and her husband wanted to move out of the trailer park and into a real house . . . someday.

Tito was a good man, treated his family well. His wife didn't suspect he would ever do anything illegal.

"Ramona's afraid Jimmy isn't coming home."

"Would that be a bad thing?" Tito asked.

"Her part time job doesn't pay enough for her and little Jimmy to live on. I know Jimmy drank away most of his income, but he made sure there was food for his family."

"Not always."

"Often enough." Linda frowned. "She may have to go on welfare."

Tito shrugged. "She won't be the first one. Besides, isn't welfare better than getting beaten all the time?"

"Isn't Jimmy your best friend?"

"I suppose."

"Why aren't you more concerned about him being missing?"

"Because ever since I found out he hit my sister, I'm not sure I want to be friends with him anymore."

Linda was relieved to hear her husband say those words. She never liked Jimmy Clay. She almost didn't marry Tito over that friendship.

"Go get washed. Supper's almost ready."

Tito obeyed, grateful the conversation had ended . . . for the time being, at least.

Chapter Eighteen

For Thursday dinner it was just Lansing and Morales. Oscar Vega was off on a date.

After nearly a year as the Lansing Ranch foreman, he had scraped together enough money to buy a used truck. He split his time between his normal duties and volunteering at Loma Amarilla Ranch. Vega was learning how to domesticate wild mustangs.

Tina had quickly thrown together a Frito pie. It was too late to start the grill, so the steaks in the refrigerator would have to wait another day.

"How bad did the fire look?" the teacher asked when they sat down at the table.

"I only have the Dome Fire to compare it with, but it looks bad. As of this evening, they estimated it's only ten percent contained."

"What does that mean, 'ten percent contained?' "

"Well, if you had a fire ten miles in circumference, but fire lines are established for only a mile along the perimeter, it would be considered ten percent contained."

"Only ten percent? After a week?"

"The winds have been fierce. They keep building fire lines, but the winds carry embers over the top of them. You understand what a fire line is, right?"

"Sure. That's where they clear vegetation out of the way to keep the fire from spreading."

Lansing nodded, then took a bite of his meal. He pointed at the plate with his fork. "This is good!"

"You sound surprised."

"If it was me cooking, we'd be trying to choke down a frozen Patio Mexican Dinner."

"I knew you only loved me for my cooking."

"The way to a man's heart." He took another bite of food.

The two ate quietly for a few minutes.

"When they can," Lansing started again, "they try to build the fire breaks using bulldozers and other heavy equipment. Another reason the fire is only partially contained is they can't get that equipment into the canyons. Nearly all the fire lines are being dug by hand. They even have to dig out the roots to keep the fire from spreading underground."

"Those poor men!"

"Women, too," the sheriff observed.

"Is nothing sacred?" Tina kidded.

"Not anymore." Lansing reached for a second helping.

"You sure you want to do that?"

He reconsidered. Since Tina moved in, he wasn't watching his caloric intake as closely as before. "Fat-and-Forty" was starting to mean something. Not putting on the weight to begin with was easier than trying to take it off. He was grateful for her discouraging extra portions.

"You're right."

Instead of dishing more, he stood and carried both of their plates to the sink.

After the table was cleared and the dishes washed, they moved into the living room. Lansing stacked kindling, then started a small blaze in the fireplace. The evenings were still cool in the high desert.

After pouring a short whiskey, he sat on the sofa. Tina joined him.

"Roberto and I are meeting at the lawyer's office in the morning along with our accountants."

"So, you really are going to sell half the ranch?" Tina asked as she sipped on wine.

"He can't afford to buy half. I brought the price down to a thousand dollars an acre, but he couldn't make the figures work. So, he's purchasing two thousand acres."

"That's still two million dollars. What are you going to do with all that money?"

"Oh, I won't see that much up front."

"Why not?"

"Because I'll be carrying the note."

"He's not going through a bank?"

"I made him an offer he couldn't refuse. I undercut the bank by two percentage points. He's going to pay me directly. Of course, I get to pay taxes on the interest. If he defaults, which I hope doesn't happen, the land reverts back to me, not to some blood-sucking bank."

"How long is the note for?"

"Twenty-five years. Obviously, he can pay it off anytime."

"Why are you so intent on selling any of the ranch?"

"C.J. told me when he graduates next year, he wants to go to the Colorado School of Mines."

"C.J.? You mean 'Cal' don't you?"

Lansing grimaced. When his son started high school, he decided he didn't want to be pegged a "Junior" all his life. He announced to his friends and family his preferred nickname from that point would be Cal . . . from the initials of his full name "Clifford Allen Lansing."

"Yeah . . . Cal. Anyway, out-of-state tuition will be about twenty-seven thousand dollars a year, not counting room and board."

"Why Colorado?"

"The School of Mines is the second highest rated engineering school in the country."

"I've heard the University of New Mexico is pretty darn good, too."

"True . . . and I mentioned that. I think he wants to get as far away from Albuquerque as he can."

"Trouble at home?"

Lansing shrugged. Carol walked out nine years earlier, taking C.J./Cal with her. The ex-husband never cared much for the new husband, Richard Enriquez. One of Carol's old high school boyfriends, he weaseled himself into her life after his own divorce. What Carol saw in the man Lansing wasn't sure. He knew his son held the same disdain for the man as he did.

"If C . . . I mean, if Cal needs my help, especially with finances, I'll be there for him."

Tina knew Lansing felt guilty over not being Cal's full-time father. He wanted to do anything he could to make up for those last nine years. She also knew Cal would never try to capitalize on that guilt. Despite the fact the C.J. didn't want to be considered a Junior, he worshiped his father.

"I know you will, Cliff." She leaned over and kissed him. "That's one of the reasons I love you."

He gladly returned the kiss. "I love you, too."

She smiled. "I know."

Chapter Nineteen

Eric Gonzales leaned his wooden chair backwards so that it rested against a tool shed. A twelve-gauge leaned against the wall as well. His wool jacket didn't keep the cool mountain air from chilling him. He sat with his arms crossed and his feet dangling. He swung them slightly.

His guard duty started at sunset and would last until sunrise . . . or until something happened.

He would graduate from Segovia High School in a week . . . a day he thought would never come. Not a great student, he was satisfied with a solid "C" average. There was no point in striving for higher grades. He was being groomed to take over the farm. As far as he knew, farmers didn't need much formal education, and he certainly wasn't going to college.

He wouldn't miss the homework and dull classes. He especially wouldn't miss the hour bus ride every morning and again every afternoon. It made for long days, especially if he had a stack of chores waiting for him when he got home.

Looking up at the dazzling stars, he suddenly felt alone. There was one thing he would miss about school. Actually, it was one person he would miss . . . Joy Baca.

Since eleventh grade, they had a school day romance going. They hung out together between classes. They had lunch together. He had taken her to Junior Prom. After the graduation ceremony, he would take here to the Senior Prom. He and his best friend, Adam Sanchez, would be double dating.

Gonzales' problem was he didn't know what would happen once school was over. He hoped farm work would keep him occupied. But there would also be moments like this . . . moments when he would be engulfed in loneliness.

Joy had missed school the day before. She had to stay home to help fire her pottery. He missed her so much his stomach hurt.

She already announced she would follow in her mother's footsteps to become a fulltime potter. Joy was smart. Much smarter than him. He had been afraid she would go off to college, so he was relieved with her chosen career path.

But Joy was down in Santa Clara Pueblo, and he was stuck in the mountains over an hour away. His family owned one vehicle . . . a truck. His father never let him use it except for farm duties. It certainly wouldn't be available for dates.

Not having a paying job, the graduating senior had no way to buy his own car.

He had never understood why Joy Baca liked him. They were the same height, but he was stocky, like his father. She was slight, almost delicate.

The big, Hispanic jocks chased after flashy Latinas. The few Anglo boys chose Anglo girls.

The Pueblo kids from San Juan and Santa Clara mostly hung out together.

Maybe Joy liked him because he wasn't a Pueblo Indian. She fortunately wasn't rejected by her peers because she dated him.

And, he mused, Pueblo men and women married people outside their villages all the time.

"Marriage?" he said out loud. "Where the hell did that come from, Gonzales?"

The thin air of the mountain valley reverberated with the sound of a gunshot. The new foliage of the trees along Cañada Creek muffled the sound slightly, but Gonzales recognized the blast as coming from a shotgun. He jumped up and looked in the direction of the sound. A moment later a second shot was fired.

A half mile away, Adam Sanchez was guarding his sheep pens, just as Gonzales was protecting the hen house.

Eric looked at his parents' farmhouse. All the lights were off.

Of course, they were. It had to be past midnight.

He debated whether or not to wake his father. Something was happening not far away, and he wanted to know what it was.

It wouldn't hurt to abandon his post. The bear couldn't be in two places at once.

He grabbed his own shotgun, then turned on his flashlight. Hurrying down the road, he swung the beam from one side to the other, looking, hoping the bear would come in his direction. That is, unless Adam had killed it already.

He must have, Eric reasoned. Why else would there be a second shot?

"Turn off that light?" a loud whisper ordered.

"Adam, is that you?"

"Who else would it be?"

Eric approached a dark silhouette. As he got closer, he recognized his best friend holding his weapon.

"Did you kill it?" Gonzales asked in a hoarse whisper.

"No, dammit." They both continued to speak in subdued tones.

"Well, did you hit it?"

"I didn't even shoot at it. It was standing in the middle of the flock. I didn't want to hit any of the sheep. I fired onto the air to scare it off."

"Was it the bear?"

"Yeah, it must have been. It was big. At least five feet tall. It was reared up on its hind legs."

"It didn't get any sheep, did it?"

"I hope not."

"Why the second shot?"

"When I fired the first time, the bear just stood there. I don't know what it was thinking. It didn't run away until after the second shot."

"I'd better get back, just in case it decides it wants a chicken dinner."

"Yeah, I'm not going anywhere. It may decide it's more hungry than afraid."

"See you in the morning." Gonzales turned to leave.

"Yeah, see ya, Eric."

Chapter Twenty

After five years, the Red Ranch Outfitters were ready to upgrade their facilities. The three partners lived in the main house, which doubled as their offices and chow hall. The two visitor's trailers were being replaced with permanent bunk houses and showers.

The business plan specified that any improvements could not be financed by more than fifty percent. The rest of the money had to come from profits. By hiring out their labor when there was no hunting, there was always a steady stream of income.

"Sorry we're so busy, Mr. Stevenson. I'm sure my dad can help . . . Sure. Talk to you later."

"What was that all about?" Ben Gallegos asked as Albert hung up the phone.

"Oh!" Cabrera looked from his partner to the phone, then back. "Ed Stevenson has a couple dozen head of cattle he needs to move closer to the reservoir. Only enough work for about half a day."

"So, Red Ranch Outfitters are too busy? I thought we all agreed, in the off season we'd take any work thrown our way."

"He's only paying fifteen dollars an hour . . . plus you have to provide your own horse. We'll make sixty bucks, tops."

Gallegos frowned. "You told Stevenson to call your dad? When did you start cutting him any slack?"

"I talked to John about it . . . I should have said something to you. My folks are going to lose their ranch. Mom asked if we could throw some work my dad's way."

"Sixty dollars is going to save them?"

"Of course not. My mom wants to keep him busy. If he's working, maybe he won't drink so much."

"That old bastard ran us all off. Did you forget that?"

There was anger and bitterness in Gallegos' words, and Albert wasn't sure the attitude was solely directed at his father.

"No, I didn't. Do you really feel like chewing some dust today? I can call Stevenson back."

"Naw, forget it." Ben paused. "Do you think Ed will really call your dad? Ray Cabrera doesn't get along with anyone."

"If Stevenson's cattle are thirsty enough, he will."

Chapter Twenty-One

Ed Stevenson watched Ray Cabrera back his horse out of the trailer. The two men had been neighbors for twenty years and simply didn't like each other.

"I'm surprised you called me," Cabrera said with a sneer as he led his horse up to the cattle pen.

Stevenson kept a civil tongue. He needed to move his steers that morning. "Yeah. When you need help, who better to ask than a neighbor?"

The rancher couldn't help but notice a strong whisky smell coming from Cabrera.

"Suppose you're right . . . We driving them up to the Rio Artiga pasture?"

Stevenson nodded. "That's about five miles. Shouldn't take more than a couple, maybe three hours."

"I suppose you want me on point."

"No, Ray. You'll be riding drag."

"Bringing up the rear?" Cabrera said in disgust. "What am I? Some greenhorn?"

"My foreman and I will be riding flank. You just need to watch out for strays."

"That's bull, Ed."

"Take it or leave it, Ray." He was sure Cabrera wouldn't back out. Just in case, though, he was willing to up the fee to twenty dollars an hour.

The old drunk stared at the ground, frowned, then nodded. "Okay. Sure, I'll ride drag."

It took him two tries to climb into the saddle. Once he was safely on his perch, he reached inside his coat and pulled out a glass pint of whiskey. When he thought no one was looking, he took a quick swig.

Stevenson didn't miss a thing. He promised himself, if Cabrera fell off his horse, no one would stop to help him.

Chapter Twenty-Two

Lansing stood at his desk sipping coffee. He had managed to find a topographical map similar to the one the State Police showed him. Referring to the most current data about the Cerro Grande Fire, he tried to pinpoint its progress.

By New Mexico standards, Los Alamos County was tiny. If it were laid out in a rectangle, it would only be ten miles by eleven miles. By contrast, the city of Albuquerque was twice as big.

The county was bordered by Frijoles Canyon on the south, Santa Clara Pueblo to the north, Rio Grande on the east, and Valles Caldera on the west.

***

Valles Caldera was the remnants of a collapsed volcano. Its last eruption was 1.2 million years ago. Numerous hot springs testified to the area's volcanic past. Almost perfectly round, the base of the structure rested 500 feet below the surrounding rim. After the last eruption and collapse, cylinder cones such as Redondo Peak built up on the crater floor. At over 11,000 feet, it was the second highest point in the Jemez Mountains. Thirteen and a half miles across, the 93,000 acres was home to the largest elk herd in New Mexico.

Human occupation began 11,000 years ago and the surrounding Pueblo people still claim certain areas as sacred. White settlement began in the early 1800s. Overgrazing by millions of sheep and cattle almost destroyed the pristine meadows and creeks. Overlogging scarred the land with roads and removed thousands of Douglas firs and ponderosa pines.

Texas rancher Pat Dunnigan bought the property in 1963 and began restoring the habitat. It took nearly thirty years for the family to negotiate the sale of the ranch to the federal government. The final purchase was to be complete by July. That Valles Caldera was spared the devastation of the Cerro Grande Fire was a miracle.

***

Six hundred and fifty firefighters from across the country were now engaged with the monster wildfire. More were being called up.

They had stopped the inferno at Highway 4, keeping the fire out of the rest of Bandelier National Monument. Winds and the mountains along the eastern rim blocked the fire from consuming the meadows and forests of the caldera.

Firefighters had struggled to save Los Alamos and the National Laboratories to the south. So far, two hundred and thirty-five homes in the town were destroyed and one hundred and twenty buildings at the National Lab had been consumed. But it appeared they had been successful in stopping further losses.

However, in protecting manmade structures, the flames escaped to the southeast and to the north. Easily half of Los Alamos County had been consumed. The fire had jumped Guaje Canyon and now pushed its way into Sandoval County and the Santa Clara Reservation.

San Phillipe was next.

The phone on Lansing's desk rang.

"Yes?"

"Sheriff, this is Marilyn. We just got a call. Someone found a dead body."

"Where?"

"A couple of miles east of Artiga, just north of Highway five-fifty. A rancher saw vultures circling and wanted to make sure he hadn't lost a calf."

He pinpointed the spot on his map from Marilyn's description.

"Make sure an ambulance has been called. Contact Deputy Trumbull. I'll need her there. And tell her I'm on my way."

Chapter Twenty-Three

Eric Gonzales, Adam Sanchez, and Jerry Landa studied the disturbed earth next to the Sanchez sheep pens. Eric and Adam managed to intercept the third senior before he headed to school. They were going after the bear that had raided the two farms.

The fact that neither Gonzales nor Sanchez had gotten much sleep the night before didn't diminish their gusto for an adventure. They knew bringing Landa along might be a risk. He was tall, gangly, and whined a lot, but they needed Landa's hunting dog for their quest.

All three teens had hunted their entire lives. Their fathers had full confidence in their abilities and trusted in their skills. They were also savvy enough to stay safe. So, despite their mothers' misgivings, the three young men were eager to hunt down the marauder.

"Are you sure that's a bear track?" Landa asked. "It doesn't look like any track I've ever seen."

"It's gotta be," Eric said. "It's too wide for a human print."

"I don't see any claw marks."

"Come on, Jerry," Sanchez argued. "They don't always show up. Especially when the ground is hard like this."

"I suppose." He turned to his German Shepherd. Chulo wasn't the greatest tracker in the world, but he never backed down. Landa pulled his dog closer to get a scent from the track.

The dog cooperated at first. Turning his head back and forth, he swept the ground for a smell he could identify.

After fifteen full seconds, Chulo stopped sniffing. The hair on his shoulders bristled and he emitted a low growl, before backing away. He looked up at Landa and whimpered.

"What ya got, boy?" Jerry asked, kneeling next to the animal. "You got a bear?"

Chulo whimpered again and pulled away from his owner.

"That has to be a bear," Adam Sanchez said, nodding. "Look how he's acting."

"Yeah." Jerry's agreement dripped with doubt.

"We need to get moving," Gonzales said, cradling his Winchester Model 70 in his arms. "Did you remember your camera?"

Adam nodded. "It's in my backpack."

The bear would probably be too big to drag out of the mountains. The camera was to provide photographic evidence they had indeed killed the animal.

Starting across the unplowed field, the three seniors followed the faint trail the predator had left. Eric and Adam carried Winchesters. Jerry had his father's Remington 700. All three wore backpacks with enough water and provisions to last a day, just in case the hunt lasted until the following morning.

The track led to an animal trail at the edge of the field. The trail led up the steep slope, weaving between the sparce juniper trees.

As the teens started the climb, Chulo stopped at the bottom.

"Come on, boy," Landa coaxed. "We have work to do."

The dog whimpered and danced nervously.

Jerry came back to his dog and knelt again. "It's okay, Chulo. It's just a bear. You've seen bears before."

Chulo licked Landa's hand and face, as if begging his master to offer a different option.

"Come on, Jerry," Adam ordered. "If your stupid dog is too chicken to hunt, leave him be."

Landa stood. "It's okay, boy. If you don't want to come, you don't have to."

He reluctantly started up the slope to join the other hunters. Occasionally, Landa looked down the hill to see if Chulo was following. The dog remained at the bottom, sitting and watching the hunting party disappear up the mountain.

The trail led them over the top of a ridge. The strip of farmland disappeared behind them. Further up, the trees thickened, and the trio realized only luck would guide them to their quarry.

Landa heard a bark. He turned to see Chulo scampering to catch up with the group.

Eric smiled. "I guess he's not a chicken after all."

Jerry knelt to welcome his friend. "That's a good boy . . ."

Chulo again licked his master's face and hands.

"I knew you wouldn't let me down." He stood. "Come on, Chulo. We need to find us a bear."

Chapter Twenty-Four

Lansing stood out of the way while Marla Trumbull took pictures.

Trumbull was hired to replace Leroy Ramirez after his twenty-two-year sentence for drug crimes. Wilma Estrada begged for the new deputy to be trained in forensics. She was being spread thin and needed the help. Trumbull was hired after completing forensics training.

Physically, Marla Trumbull was intimidating. At five-foot, eleven inches tall, she towered over Estrada. In fact, she was taller than most of the other deputies. An athlete all her life, she easily conjured up the image of an Amazon Warrior. Her boss suspected she could outrun and outwrestle any man in their office.

She wore her blonde hair pulled back tight with little makeup . . . something she didn't need, anyway. The whole package was pleasingly attractive, and she had little problem finding dates.

It appeared the man's body had been tossed from the dirt road twenty feet above the arroyo. Whether the fall caused the death was still to be determined.

Scavengers had been feasting on the remains. Coyotes, crows and vultures each took their turn, leaving bones exposed. Landing in such a fashion that his left hand was protected by his body, Trumbull could get fingerprints. That was fortunate because except for a set of keys no other form of identification could be found.

"I'm ready for you to turn him over," the deputy said to the two paramedics.

Trumbull took more pictures. The front of the shirt was stained with dried blood. Embarrassed at the thought, the sheriff half-hoped this man was the source of the bloody asphalt behind the Western Auto. It would tie up loose ends neatly.

Once Trumbull was finished gathering evidence, the victim was placed in a body bag and carried up the hill.

While the dead man was being transported to Albuquerque for an autopsy, both the sheriff and his deputy scoured the bottom of the arroyo for more clues to the man's identity.

Neither mentioned the imposing tower of smoke billowing fifteen miles to the south. After a week, the Cerro Grande Fire had attained a measure of permanence. People wondered if that smudge across the blue New Mexico skies would ever go away.

It was nearly noon before Lansing and his deputy reached their vehicles.

"There's a restaurant a few miles south of here. I'm going to get some lunch. Care to join me?" Lansing asked.

The deputy secured her forensics kit in her unit. "Dead bodies make you hungry?"

"With this job, you eat whenever you can. You don't know when you'll get stuck a hundred miles from the nearest café."

"I suppose it serves Mexican food," Trumbull sighed.

"This is New Mexico," Lansing smiled. "What would you expect?"

"Don't get me wrong," Trumbull explained. "Mexican food's all right, but I grew up in Roswell. I think we had Taco Bell and one other Mexican restaurant. The rest were barbeque joints or steak houses. That's what I was raised on."

"They do have pizza on the menu."

"Oh, that's okay. I'll eat whatever's available." She opened the door to her patrol car. "Ever had armadillo?"

Lansing crinkled his nose. "No. Is it any good?"

"Not as good as possum . . . at least that's what I heard." She slid into her seat and closed the door.

Getting into his Jeep, Lansing glanced back at her and scratched the back of his neck. He suspected he had just been had by a rookie.

Chapter Twenty-Five

Joy Baca hung up the telephone and walked into the dining room. She looked unhappy.

"Why the frown?" her mother asked, looking up from her clay.

"I called Eric to see why he wasn't at school today. His mother said he had gone hunting with two other boys from my class."

"That's unusual, isn't it. Couldn't they wait until this weekend?"

"I guess not. They're having trouble with a bear killing their animals. They want to stop it before it comes back."

Dorothy stopped her project to look at her daughter. "Isn't that dangerous? I mean, shouldn't their fathers do the hunting?"

"I don't know about the others, but Eric's been hunting since he was twelve. His dad probably thinks he can handle himself. Besides, it's not like he's out in the mountains by himself."

"So, why are you worried?"

"I'm not," she said, shrugging. "It's just, after next week, I'm not sure how much we'll see each other."

Dorothy Baca nodded. Joy and the Gonzales boy had dated for two years. Teenage romances came and went. She was sure the infatuation would wear off once they graduated and went their separate ways. Besides, she had always hoped her daughter would settle down with a nice pueblo boy and live close to her family.

"He's not going away to school, is he?"

"Eric? No. He's going to work on the family farm."

Trying to change the subject, Dorothy nodded at the mound of clay she was kneading to remove air pockets. "Are you going to start a new project this weekend?"

"I don't know." Joy sat in a chair opposite her mother and stared out the window. "Aren't they ever going to put out that fire?"

"I'm sure they will. Why don't you turn on the TV to see if they're talking about it?"

"What channel?"

"Try seven."

Santa Fe had no television stations. Albuquerque carried the three major networks with coverage for local news. Though evening news wasn't scheduled for another hour, the ABC affiliate was doing its best to provide continuing updates on the Cerro Grande Fire.

A video of the fire appeared on the screen. It was a long shot of tall ponderosa pines engulfed in flames. The video cut to a dozen firefighters digging a trench on a slope, constructing a fire break.

"These are only a handful of the heroes battling this catastrophic inferno," a voice said in the background. "Some of them have been on the line since last weekend, working sixteen hours a day."

The video cut to a reporter holding a microphone. He wore an orange hazard vest over a plaid shirt and a red hard hat. Next to him was a Forest Service firefighter. His hard hat was dark green with a US Forest Service emblem on the side. His long-sleeved yellow shirt was smeared with black residue from the fire. He had wiped his face clean for the interview, but it was obvious he had not shaved in days.

A curtain of fire and smoke only a quarter of a mile away served as a backdrop.

"With me is wildland firefighter Alex Redmond. Alex, I understand you and your crew are from Silver City?"

"That's right. We're assigned to the Gila National Forest, but we go where we're needed."

"How long have you been here at Los Alamos?"

"We got the call when a Type One Wildfire Emergency was declared on Monday. We drove all night and arrived at the Base Camp in time for the morning briefing. Today will be our fourth day on the line."

"Where exactly has your crew operated?"

"Initially, we were working north of Frijoles Canyon, but yesterday they moved us east to Water Canyon. They needed a barrier between the fire and White Rock."

"Is your fire break holding?"

"It has, so far.

"How long do you anticipate you and your crew will have to stay?"

"As long as it takes."

"So, no idea."

"No idea." He looked over his shoulder. "I need to get back to work."

"Thank you for your time, Alex." The reported looked into the camera. "There will be a complete update on the Cerro Grande Fire at our five o'clock broadcast.

"This is Robert Angelo reporting from Los Alamos County."

From behind Joy, her brother said, "Yeah, they'll be there for as long as it takes."

"How long is that?"

"Hell, if I know. This was going to be my first big fire."

Lincoln walked past his sister and out the front door. The look on his face summed up his mood . . . anger and frustration.

Joy could see him through the screen door, staring into the distance, watching the smoke from a fire less than ten miles away.

Chico had followed him outside. He sat patiently waiting for his best friend to offer a friendly scratch. When none came, he laid down, his head on his paws. He sensed he would have to wait until Lincoln's sullenness passed.

Chapter Twenty-Six

New Mexico is divided into three natural regions: The Interior Plains, The Intermontane Plateaus and The Rocky Mountain System. The Interior Plains comprises the eastern one third of the state and extends from Texas north to Colorado. The Intermontane Plateau region is the largest with two areas: The Colorado Plateau in the northwest and The Basin and Range Provence south of Santa Fe.

The Rocky Mountain System, at nine thousand square miles, takes up less than eight percent of the state. This system is broken down into four sub ranges: Sangre de Cristo Mountains along the eastern side, Tusas Mountains between Las Palmas and Taos, Sierra Nacimiento on the southwest, and the Jemez Mountains which contains Los Alamos, Valles Caldera and Bandelier National Monument.

***

The three teenagers knew what to expect when they started up the first slope. The Jemez Mountains were typical of a lot of western ranges. The leeward on the eastern side of the mountains was drier than the windward side. As the air was pushed up a mountain, the moisture was squeezed out, released as rain. The result was thicker, lusher vegetation on the western slopes.

Initially, the trail wandered between juniper trees stunted from sparce rains. The top of the mesa was six hundred feet above the farms. Once there, Jerry Landa and Chulo took the lead. The trail was less defined, and the dog's olfactory senses were needed.

Chulo led them through a thick stand of forest. After a short while, the trail made a turn to the south and east. Soon they found themselves going down a steep, treeless slope, approaching Cañada Creek, the same creek that ran through their farms.

"Does that dog of yours know where he's going?" Eric asked.

"You're the ones who wanted him on this little trip," Jerry snapped. "He didn't ask to come along."

"All right, all right."

After descending to the canyon floor, Chulo lost the scent at the bank of the creek. The water was only a few feet across and ten inches deep.

"We're about two miles from my farm," Eric observed. He watched the dog search to the left and right along the bank, trying to find the scent again. "Let's take him to the other side . . . see if he can pick up the trail there."

Jerry nodded. "Come on Chulo." Landa jumped the two feet to the opposite bank, then turned back to his dog. "Come on, boy."

Chulo hesitated, then leapt. He cleared the water with no difficulty.

The other two hunters joined them.

Landa knelt and patted the ground. "Okay, boy, let's find that bear again."

The trail Chulo followed was in thick woods. The dark forest became even darker. All three boys had hunted throughout this part of the Jemez Mountains. They knew they could find their way home with no difficulty.

Heading east, they followed animal trails and crossed a seldom used dirt road. The progress was slow. Chulo would follow the scent for thirty or forty feet, lose it, then pick it up again.

"Can you believe all the deer we've seen?" Adam asked when they came across their third cluster of animals. The deer scampered away quickly when they approached.

"It's that fire," Eric observed. "They're being driven north. Everything in the forest is trying to get out of its way."

They crossed a mesa, went down a ravine, only to climb up the other side.

"Where the hell is this stupid bear going?" Adam Sanchez groused.

He said the same thing the other two seniors were thinking.

"Probably isn't even the same bear," Eric added.

"We can quit any time you want," Jerry said. "To tell you the truth, I'm getting tired."

The three stopped to rest at the edge of a clearing. Landa gave Chulo some water from his bottle, then took a swig himself. It was late afternoon. The sun was beyond the western peaks, and the darkening mesa was getting chilly.

Eric and Adam looked at each other, exchanging the same thought . . . how could they quit with nothing to show for their effort?

Jerry could care less. Landa was about to suggest they head home, when he heard the sound of wood knocking against a tree. Chulo emitted a low growl. Jerry shushed the other two.

"What is it Chulo?" Landa asked in a hoarse whisper. He looked across the small meadow in the direction the dog was staring. He asked the others, "Did you hear that knocking?"

"Yeah," Adam said.

All three studied the thick forest to their east. There was movement.

The shadow of a lone figure stepped out from behind a tree.

Adam raised his rifle, attempting to focus the sight on the target.

"It's not an elk, is it?" Eric whispered.

"No. It's not big enough."

"It's not some hiker?" Jerry asked

"Whatever it is, it's not wearing clothes. I think it's the bear."

Eric raised his rifle to draw a bead as well. "What do you think? Fifty, sixty yards?"

"Yeah." Adam agreed. He released the safety with his right thumb without taking his eye off the quarry. He took a deep breath, slowly let it out, then squeezed the trigger.

The quiet forest echoed with the sound of the rifle's blast.

The dark figure let out a shriek that shook the three men to their souls. It took one step, then disappeared.

Chapter Twenty-Seven

"That wasn't a bear!" Jerry Landa said softly. Chulo stood next to him barking.

"What the hell did you just shoot?" Eric asked. The question was barely a whisper.

"I don't know." Adam Sanchez's voice quavered. He snapped at Landa in a hoarse whisper, "Keep your damned dog quiet, would ya!"

"I'm trying."

All three teens stood frozen, unsure what to do next.

"We need to check it out," Gonzalez said without much conviction.

"Yeah, I guess we should." Sanchez's voice registered just as much doubt.

The two of them took hesitant steps. Landa stayed behind, finally quieting his dog.

Halfway across the meadow, the two hunters noticed the forest around them was quiet. Too quiet.

Suddenly they heard the knocking of wood against a tree. Three distinct knocks. They stopped and shushed each other.

The knocks came a second time. They seemed close.

No one moved. No one said a thing.

Then came the crash of a tree falling. The surrounding forest was filled with a howl . . . a deep, long howl that sent shivers down their spines.

"What the hell was that?" Landa asked in a loud whisper behind them.

"I don't know," Sanchez said.

Chulo whimpered. The other two teens shook their heads. It didn't resemble the catlike screech of a mountain lion. It was too deep to be a coyote. There were no wolves in New Mexico and bears didn't howl . . . they roared. If anything, it almost sounded human.

There came the unmistaken sound of thick branches being snapped.

"Something's coming!" Landa sounded frantic.

"We need to get out of here!" Eric broke into a run. Adam was right behind him.

"Come on Chulo, let's go home." Landa said, pulling on his dog's collar.

The three hunters grabbed their backpacks. Adam made sure his rifle was ready to be fired, just in case.

Eric signaled the others to follow him. "We came in this way."

The teens hurried in the direction they had come from. In the failing sunlight, the trail they followed disappeared in the growing darkness.

From the meadow they had just abandoned came another howl. It was different from the first one. This one was longer, sharper, awash in anguish.

"My God," Eric said. "What have we done?"

Chapter Twenty-Eight

Dorothy Gonzales stood on the back porch, staring at the side of Cañada Mesa. Her son, Eric, and the other two boys had started up the steep slope around eight that morning. The sun was setting, though the deep valley had been engulfed in shadows since 4:00 that afternoon.

To the south, the sky was lit with an orange glow. It looked like the lights from a big city, but the worried mother knew better.

The evening mountain air was chilly, and a shiver ran through her. She stepped back into the warmth of the kitchen.

Esteban looked up from the farming magazine he was reading. "There is no reason to be worried, Dot. Those boys know how to handle themselves."

"I don't like them out there after dark. I don't think they even wore coats."

Without looking up from her coloring book, Edith said, "Eric took his blue jacket."

The parents looked at each other. Edie seemed to always know what was happening around the farm.

"Are you sure?" Dorothy asked.

"Uh huh. He put it in his backpack. He took a flashlight, too."

"Well, there. See?" Esteban said to his wife. "Eric knew they might be in the woods after dark."

"What about the fire?" she protested.

"It's twenty miles away."

"Not any more . . . The news said it crossed into Santa Clara Pueblo. That's only fifteen miles away."

"I doubt they'd chase a bear that far . . ."

The phone rang in the living room. Dorothy rushed to answer it.

"Hello?"

She listened for a moment, then signaled to her husband. "Vernon wants to talk to you."

Esteban got up from the table and took the receiver when his wife handed it to him.

"Hi, Vern. Did they boys get back?"

He listened for a moment, then repeated the answer so his wife would know.

"So, they're not back yet. Yeah, sure. If they show up here, I'll let you know. . . Yeah, sure. I'll call the Landas and let them know, too. Talk to you later."

Dorothy couldn't hide her concern. "Is Jean as worried about the boys as me?"

"I don't doubt that she is," he said hanging up the phone. "You mothers are all the same."

"What are we going to do if they don't get home tonight?"

"Nothing we can do. If they're not home by noon, we can go looking for them."

Edie looked up from her artwork. "Oh! Can I go?"

"No, you can't!" Dorothy said in a tone that eliminated any chance of argument.

"No, honey," her father said. "You'd be worn out before we got to the top of the mesa. You'd be begging to go home."

"No, I wouldn't," the four-year-old pouted.

"Yes, you would," Dorothy confirmed. "Now go watch TV with the others. I think the *Cosby* show is coming on. I need to clean the kitchen."

"Okay." Edith got out of her seat and started for the living room.

"And take your mess with you."

Edie pouted as she scooped up her crayons and coloring book.

Chapter Twenty-Nine

While grilling steaks, Lansing and Morales shared their activities for the day.

For Tina, there were four days of school left before the summer vacation started. All her students seemed to be marking time until the final bell. She had opted out of teaching summer school. She felt she needed the time off.

She had asked Lansing if he minded her spending a large chunk of her vacation in Phoenix and Nogales, Mexico. Since reuniting with her best friend from high school, Charlotte Etsitty, she wanted to get to know her two daughters better.

She also needed to dedicate a few weeks to seeing her grandmother. Her *abuela* was turning ninety. The teacher wanted to absorb as much knowledge as she could about being a *curendera* before that fount of knowledge passed on.

Although Lansing knew he would miss her, he also knew he couldn't expect her to isolate herself on the ranch or in Las Palmas. That was what drove his wife away eight years earlier. To save two long days of driving, he offered to cover her plane fare, which she readily accepted. Her car, Midnight, was getting old and might not last the entire trip.

The sheriff glossed over his activities that day. He didn't mention the body in the arroyo.

It wasn't a pleasant topic just before eating. Their discussion mostly centered around the Cerro Grande Fire and guesses about what would happen.

***

"Sheriff, I was wondering," Oscar Vega asked after a second bite of steak, "Do you think I can bed my own horse here at the ranch?"

"A horse from Loma Amarilla?"

Vega nodded.

"One of the horses you 'gentled?' " Tina asked.

Loma Amarilla Ranch was a sanctuary for Montero Mustangs . . . the descendants of the horses introduced by the Spanish. Started a year earlier, the caretakers only accepted rescues with a high percentage of original DNA markers. After twelve months, the herd had grown from twenty-five horses to over fifty. Some were from other wild herds, the others, newborns.

It was decided the ranch could only accommodate two hundred horses. To preclude sending the older horses to slaughterhouses, a "gentling" program was instituted to domesticate the feral animals. That way they could be offered safely to the public.

Since its inception, Oscar had volunteered at the ranch to learn how to handle wild horses. He had decided after working on Lansing's ranch through high school that he wanted train horses for a living.

Vega nodded again. "Dr. Beltran says it's a three-year-old."

"A three-year-old male?" Lansing asked.

"Yeah, but the doc says he can geld it. It would be easier to control him in the long run."

Lansing pondered the request. The barn had four stalls. Three were occupied with Cement Head, Paladin, and Little Orphan Annie. The fourth was used for storage.

"You'll need to clear out that extra stall," the rancher observed. "We'll also have to figure out your share of feed costs."

"Oh, I can work that off," Vega said eagerly. "I have it all figured out." He pulled a folded sheet of paper from his back pocket.

"That's all right," Lansing assured him. "We'll discuss it later . . . after we eat."

"Okay." Vega smiled and resumed eating with gusto.

"How was your date last night?" Tina cringed at her own question. She was afraid she sounded like a mother hen.

"It was good," Oscar admitted. "We couldn't go out tonight or tomorrow night because she has to work."

"Where?" Lansing asked casually.

"*The High Desert Restaurant* . . . she's a waitress."

"One of my old students?" Morales asked.

"Actually, she's in your class this year," the ranch foreman nodded. "Maria Alba."

"I thought, after she was abducted last year, she never wanted to work there again?"

Vega shrugged. "She must have changed her mind. She's working there now."

"I didn't know you two were dating," the chemistry teacher admitted.

"Just that one date last night."

"Is Maria your first girl friend?"

"She's the first one I could afford to take on a date in my own car." The admission was almost painful. "She's working so she can take classes this fall. She's going to Northern New Mexico College in Segovia. She said she'll have to commute, so she's saving up for a car."

"That's only a two-year school. Do you know if she's going to transfer so she can get a four-year degree?"

Vega let out a deep sigh. "I hope not. I don't want her to move away."

Lansing thought about saying something sage like, "Don't worry . . . She may be your first, but she probably won't be your last."

He realized he'd better not. He wanted Tina Morales to be his last partner for the rest of his life. He didn't want to say something that might infer he thought differently.

Instead, he nodded. "She's a nice girl."

"She is . . . plus she says she likes horses."

"You should bring her out riding," Lansing suggested.

"I can do that?"

"You live here, too, Oscar, so, of course you can."

Chapter Thirty

"Listen, I have job lined up tomorrow after work," Tito said, looking up from his plate. "I'm not sure when I'll get home."

The next day was Saturday. *Luis' Car Repair and Body Shop* closed at noon.

"I was going to suggest we take a drive," Linda said, pouting. "We all need to get away from this smoke. It's not good for the boys."

"Yeah, yeah, I know." Calle agreed the smoke from the Cerro Grande Fire couldn't be healthy for anyone. What smoke didn't reach the ground hung like a shroud over all of Segovia, blocking the sun. He thought hard for a solution. "Well, if Jimmy isn't home yet, why don't you and Ramona use her car and take off for the day. You won't have to wait till I got off work."

His wife nodded slowly. "Yes, I guess that would work. Where should we go? Artiga Lake?"

"No, no. I wouldn't go there." Artiga Reservoir was in the same direction as his hidden truck. He didn't want to accidently encounter his family on the road. "Why don't you go to Santa Fe and see a movie? The *Cinema 6* oughta have something the kids can watch."

"That sounds good. I think that new Flintstones movie is out."

"If Ramona is worried about money, tell her we'll pay for everything." The suggestion was to placate his own guilt. "You can all go to *McDonalds* for lunch."

"That's a good idea. Feed them before the movie so we don't buy junk food at the theater."

"Really?" Juan, their oldest squealed. "We're going to the movies!"

He grabbed his brother and they both jumped up and down in their chairs, knocking over a glass of milk.

"Dammit!" Tito snapped. "See what you did? Calm down or you're not going anywhere tomorrow."

"It's all right," Linda said, using paper napkins to stop the spreading milk. "They're just excited."

"We're sorry!" Roberto said. Going to the movies was a rare treat and the five-year-old was afraid they had blown their chance.

"Yes, we're sorry." Juan held back tears.

"It's okay," their mother said calmly. "Don't cry over spilt milk . . . Isn't that what they always say?" She shot her husband a stern look.

"Yeah, boys," Tito agreed, smiling. "It's just spilled milk."

Chapter Thirty-One

Jerry Landa became physically awkward when he turned thirteen and began to grow taller. While other boys adapted to their entry into manhood, Landa never did. He was *un estorbo*, an embarrassment, to his teammates no matter what sport he tried. He looked ridiculous when he tried to run.

The three hunters hurried down the slope, putting distance between themselves and the "thing" they probably killed. Following their original trail was impossible in the growing darkness. All three stumbled in the thick undergrowth, but Landa struggled the most. Even though he fell further behind, Chulo stayed at his side.

Almost to the bottom of the canyon, Eric looked first at Adam, then at the dark woods behind him.

"Where's Jerry?"

Adam looked at the way they had just come. "Crap, I thought he was behind me!"

He cupped his hands next to his mouth to form a megaphone and yelled, "Jerry! Where are you?"

Eric joined in. "Jerry! Are you coming?"

They stopped their hollering to listen for a response. They didn't hear anything from their companion, but they could hear Chulo barking. The sound came from one hundred and fifty feet above them.

"We need to go get him," Eric said.

Sanchez hesitantly agreed. "All right. If we have to."

"We have to," Eric said firmly, starting back up the slope.

It took a few minutes to find the barking Chulo and his master.

Jerry sat holding his ankle.

"What happened?" Adam demanded.

"What do you think?" Landa winced. "I tripped!"

"Is it broken?"

"I hope not!"

"Can you stand up?" Gonzalez asked.

"I don't know."

"You'd better." Eric looked up the slope. Another howl came from the meadow they had just left twenty minutes earlier. If anything, it sounded closer. "Come on, we'll help you up!"

The two other hunters grabbed a hand and pulled. All three struggled to get him on his feet. They were encumbered by backpacks, rifles, and the slope.

Landa cried out as they pulled him up.

"Try walking," Sanchez ordered. It was too dark for him to notice the nasty look Landa gave him.

Jerry took a step and almost collapsed. He would have fallen further down the slope if Eric hadn't caught him.

"Dammit, Jerry! Are we going to have to carry you?"

"I just need some support. I can keep going."

Gonzalez handed his rifle to Sanchez. "I'll help him."

"Whatever."

Landa was four inches taller than the other two teens. Gonzalez had no problem getting under his shoulder. It took several steps before they could establish a clumsy stride with Jerry using his rifle for a cane.

Sanchez led the way, using his flashlight to illuminate the path. His own carbine was slung over his shoulder with a strap. He had to use Eric's rifle to push branches aside.

Their progress was awkward and slow, but they finally reached the bottom of the canyon.

"Now what?" Adam asked.

"What do you mean?" Eric helped Landa sit so they both could rest.

"Do we keep going the same way, or do we follow this canyon north? It'll be easier if we go north."

"Not if this is one of those blind canyons. We'll be boxed in and have to turn around. I say we keep going till we hit that old dirt road, then turn north."

Sanchez was tired and hungry. He sat and opened his backpack. He scrounged around for a moment, looking for a sandwich. "I don't know why we're even running," he growled. "We have rifles. We can protect ourselves."

"Protect ourselves?" Gonzalez frowned, glancing up the slope they just descended. "We don't even know what's up there."

"Or how many," Jerry added.

Eric retrieved his own light from his pack and shined it toward Landa. "What do you think, Jerry? Head up to the next mesa or stay in the canyon?"

In the beam, the tall teen's face registered pain and weariness.

"I don't care." He squinted with the light in his eyes. "The canyon, I guess. It'll be easier for me." He looked toward the slope behind him. "Are you guys sure we're even being followed?"

The top of the mesa was five hundred feet above them. As if in response to the question, they heard the sound of thick branches and saplings being broken and snapped. A moment later a howl and snarl came from the darkness, followed by a crash.

Chulo started barking.

Adam jumped up, dropping his sandwich and slinging his rifle onto his shoulder.

"Yes," he said with force. "We're being followed."

Eric helped Jerry to his feet without saying a word. They followed Adam's sweeping flashlight beam as he headed north, along the rock-strewn canyon floor.

Chapter Thirty-Two

When Albert Cabrera pulled into the *Lobo Creek Market* parking lot, he immediately spotted his father's truck.

His two partners had hired out to mend broken barbed wire fences for a week. Even though it was Saturday, ranching was a seven-day-a-week proposition. Grazing livestock didn't use calendars. Albert was tasked with manning the office and answering phones. As grueling as fence work could be, it was better than being stuck inside.

Albert supposedly drew the short straw, but he didn't believe that for one second. He knew his best buddies were conspiring against him. He had overheard John and Benjamin discussing the ranch's future. It sounded like they had decided he had outlived his usefulness. The Cabrera name was needed initially to draw former clients from *Rancho Cazador*. After five years the *Red Ranch Outfitters* were on their way to being established and reliable hunting guides.

The other two partners thought a two-way split was a reasonable excuse to squeeze him out. They discussed buying his third of the business. They also hinted that there were other ways to be rid of him if he refused to sell. Albert's imagination filled in the blanks.

While repairing fences, they were probably finalizing their plans against him. He needed to make plans of his own.

The trip to the market was to pick up a few items he needed. The last thing he needed was to run into Ray Cabrera. He sat in his truck for a long moment debating whether to go inside or wait until his father left.

For five years the two Cabrera men went out of their ways to avoid each other. Their few encounters were conducted in cold silence.

"This is stupid," Albert said out loud, shutting off his engine. If his father ignored him, so be it. He was used to it.

As he shut his door, Ray stepped out of the store. The plastic bag he carried had few items. The son could guess what they were. He also noted the older man's limp.

"Have trouble with those heifers yesterday?" Albert tried to sound friendly. He even smiled.

Ray gave his son a stern look. "What are you talking about?"

When Bess Cabrera asked her son to throw work in his father's direction, she didn't want her husband to know. For sure, Ray would have turned it down. Worse, he might have slapped her around for making him seem like a charity case.

Albert thought quickly. "Mom mentioned you went to help Ed Stevenson drive some cattle yesterday. It looks like you got kicked or something."

"Why were you talking to her?" Ray asked suspiciously.

"Because she's my mom, Ray. Why else would I talk to her?"

The elder Cabrera was taken aback by Albert's defiant response. He still viewed his son as a submissive teen who was living under his roof. He wasn't sure how to address this new confidence. He failed to appreciate the idea that his son was a grown man who could stand up for himself.

"You talking about this limp I got?" Ray said, trying to sound pleasant. "Horse threw me yesterday. Probably saw a snake."

"Ah," was all Albert said. He didn't buy the explanation but went along with the lie. Ray had fallen off horses before and whiskey was the only mitigating factor in most of them.

"It seems the Andersons from Tulsa signed up with you for the fall hunt."

"Seems, so," Albert nodded. It was his turn to be surprised. This was the longest conversation they'd had in years.

"Works out for me. I was overbooked as it was." He honestly didn't suspect his son would know better. Bess wouldn't dare reveal how bad things really were.

"That's, uh, good to hear, Ray."

Cabrera cleared his throat. "Gotta get back to the ranch. Slap some new paint on that old sign."

"Okay," Albert nodded. "Say hi to mom for me."

"Yeah, will do."

Albert watched his father drive away.

Why was the old man talking to him? He had actually been friendly . . . that is, if one considered a generally sour disposition as friendly.

Would this be a new chapter?

He doubted it. In their brief encounter, Albert didn't get a whiff of alcohol. That was why his father had been civilized. He was sober.

Chapter Thirty-Three

It was a mile and a quarter from the Baca house to Santa Clara Bridge Road. The intersection was busy. Highway 15/285 came from the north and had to turn left to cross the bridge before continuing south. County Road 2 approached from the southwest. State Road 30 converged from the south and either began or ended at that traffic light, depending on one's point-of-view.

Lincoln walked through the quieter pueblo streets until Fog Road terminated at Highway 30. It was still three-quarters of a mile to the Dollar Store around the corner at the bridge road. Five hundred feet short of the intersection, a fancy rendition of the city seal welcomed visitors to Segovia.

The *Kha'po* Tewa people had lived in the area for at least eight hundred years. They moved closer to the Rio Grande around 1550 and established *Kha'po Owingeh,* rechristened Santa Clara Pueblo by the invading Spanish. The Pueblo was only two square miles, but their total reservation covered eighty square miles. Already the largest Pueblo reservation in the state, another ten square miles would be added once the Baca Ranch/Valles Caldera deal was finalized.

Lincoln couldn't help but wonder how much of their new forest had been scorched. All the reservation land west of Highway 30 was now off limits because of the fire. It was impossible for him to contain his frustration. He should have been with his comrades, fighting that fire.

Despite his injuries, he decided to not sit around and get soft and fat. He also tried not to let the smoke bother him when he went walking every day. His mother advised him to wear a bandana across his face. With a broken arm it was impossible to tie one in place. Besides it made him look as though he was going to rob someone.

He waved at the Pueblo Police truck as it passed him, heading south. The patrolman was a high school classmate, Ed Naranjo. Naranjo had always been quiet and reserved, so Baca was surprised he became a cop. He was anything but intimidating. Maybe that was a good thing. Who needed intimidating policemen?

There were fifteen cars and trucks in the Dollar Store parking lot. To Baca, that wasn't unusual. This was the closest store to the Pueblo, and it sold everything from milk to clothing. The next closest retail establishment was across the river and more than a mile away.

The three biggest sellers at the store were soft drinks, potato chips and diapers. Lincoln opted for the first two.

Two of the three checkout counters were open. They both had five customers standing in line.

Baca patiently waited his turn. When he reached the front of the line, he set the handheld basket on the counter and removed his items.

Serita Silva smiled from behind the register and did her best to bat her eyes alluringly. "Hi, Lincoln." The greeting was syrupy sweet.

"Hi, Serita," Lincoln nodded, embarrassed at the attention.

Serita was one of Joy's classmates and had made no secret she had a crush on him. She had even hinted to his sister on more than one occasion she needed an escort to the graduation prom. His injury was the perfect excuse to avoid the issue.

Silva had found another date, but that had hardly diminished her attraction to the fireman.

"It's terrible what happened to you," she said, pouting. "I am so sorry. If there is anything I can do to help . . ."

"Yes, there is," he said impatiently. "Ring me up so I can get out of here."

"Okay," she said, running his two items across a scanner. "That'll be a dollar eighty-five." She put the can of soda and the chips into a plastic bag.

He paid for his purchase. "Thanks."

"Lincoln, I really mean it," she begged. "If you need anything . . . If you need me to drive you anywhere, just call me. Joy has my number."

"All right." He pushed the door open and stepped outside.

He wasn't sure why he resisted the girl. She was slim and pretty . . . and available, it seemed.

That was it. She was too available. She wasn't a challenge. He didn't have to pursue her. He couldn't explain to himself how that made her less than attractive, but in his still adolescent mind, it did.

Chapter Thirty-Four

Lansing came into the kitchen to retrieve a cup of coffee. Tina was bent over at the oven, pulling out a pan of biscuits. It was when she stood that she spotted her partner.

"You're wearing your uniform!"

"I am," he nodded, adding milk to his coffee.

"I thought we were going to Santa Fe today."

"Well," he hedged, giving her a kiss. "I said we could look at going to Santa Fe."

"What happened between dinner last night and breakfast this morning?"

"I got a call while I was shaving. Danny Cortez's wife went into labor last night."

"Really! I didn't know it was her time already." She scowled. "You could have started off our conversation with that news."

"I guess men prioritize things differently than women," the sheriff said sheepishly.

"Who would have guessed? Do you know if it was a girl or a boy?"

He shook his head. "All I know is she went into labor. They must be at the clinic.

"At any rate, I need to cover his patrol today. You can still go to the big town without me."

"It won't be as much fun." She thought for a moment. "I know. I'll ask Marta Gomez if she'd like to do some shopping."

"See, you don't even need me."

"That's not true." She stepped closer so she could wrap her arms around his neck and give him a long, lingering kiss. "I will always need you."

Before he could answer, Tina turned her attention to the bacon fry-ing in a skillet. "I think Oscar's out at the barn. Can you tell him break-fast is almost ready?"

"I will . . ." He hesitated at the door, trying to come up with the correct response to her statement about always needing him.

She noticed his pause. It tickled her that a man so sure of himself could still struggle with terms of intimacy.

"I . . ." he started to say.

Tina smiled and nodded. "It's okay."

He smiled back, glad they could communicate without words.

Chapter Thirty-Five

Tito Calle nervously watched the office door. He was supposed to be changing spark plugs on a customer's car. Instead, he was on the phone, desperately trying to find a place to unload three sets of stolen mag wheels. Jimmy Clay supposedly had a buyer arranged before they hit the *Western Auto*. Calle had no clue who that buyer was and now had to unload them himself.

He thought Luis would be interested, but that hope was dashed when he walked into the shop that morning.

"Tito," Ramis barked, "anyone try to sell us mag wheels, you tell me about it."

"W-what do you mean?"

"Somebody broke into the *Western Auto* up in Las Palmas earlier this week. Walked off with three sets of alloy wheels. I don't deal with stolen property, so you let me know. I'll call the sheriff's office."

"Sure, Luis. Whatever you say."

Tito didn't know how Ramis found out about the theft, but if he knew about it, every other garage in San Phillipe County probably knew as well. Fortunately, his boss had a state-wide directory of repair shops and customizing outfits.

Calle was calling Albuquerque businesses. It was possible no one there had heard about the robbery. The first four places he called were not interested. Carla Perez was. They quickly settled on a price.

"Tito, what the hell are you doing on the phone?" Ramis snapped, throwing open the door. "Are you finished with those plugs?"

Calle put his hand over the receiver.

"I'm almost finished! One more minute, Luis," he pleaded. "I'm getting directions."

"One minute," the owner growled.

Tito spoke into the phone. "I've got, 'get off the interstate at Candelaria and take a right.' Then what?"

He listened for a moment, then repeated the directions. "Go down a mile, then right on fourth street. Go another two blocks, we're on the left. Got it!

"I should be there by five."

Calle hung up the phone. *Carla's Custom Cars and Trucks* didn't ask where the wheels came from. Carla didn't even balk at his asking price; she only wanted assurances he could deliver them that day.

He tore the sheet from the yellow pad on Luis' desk and headed through the door.

"All done, Luis!" he called.

"I don't know what that call was about," Ramis yelled back. "But no more doing your business on my phone. Understand?"

"Right, right," the mechanic agreed.

"Good," Luis growled. "You heard from your worthless brother-in-law yet?"

"No."

"When you see him, tell him don't come here . . . not even for his check. I don't want to see his ugly face. Tell him I'll mail him his money. Got it!"

"Yeah, sure," Calle agreed. He headed back to the car he was working on.

Chapter Thirty-Six

The smoke from the Cerro Grande Fire southeast of *Mesa de Medio* left the sun a hazy orb. It was a sight none of the teens could see from the bottom of Little Creek Canyon at the base of the mesa. However, after a night of tumbles, falls, and wrong turns, daylight was a welcome relief.

The dry bed tied into *Cañones Creek* just south of the Gonzalez farm. Despite his injury, Eric was in better shape than his two companions. He was going for help.

He half-stumbled, half-tripped most of the way. His rifle was a nuisance, but he didn't dare lose it. He had dropped it a dozen times. It now was in desperate need of cleaning. He was positive, though, it had saved his life that night.

***

After leaving the meadow, the threesome followed the dry creek bed a quarter mile to the north. The canyon suddenly split. In the darkness, it was impossible to tell which direction was best.

Adam Sanchez pointed his flashlight beam to the right. "I say we go this way."

"All right," Gonzalez agreed. "Keep moving." He shifted Landa's weight into a more comfortable position.

The ground became steeper. Three hundred yards later the canyon walls converged and became nearly vertical. They had turned up a feeder creek. It was a dead-end canyon, the kind Eric warned about earlier.

"We need to go back." Adam sounded frustrated.

"Can we sit down and rest, first?" Jerry begged.

"Not a problem." Eric was glad to be relieved of his burden.

The three sat in silence for a long moment. The only sound was Landa unzipping his backpack to find a bottle of water. Chulo lay next to him with his head on his paws.

A "Sh-h-h" came from Adam.

"What?" Jerry snapped in a harsh whisper. "I don't hear anything."

"Sh-h-h!" Adam warned again.

All three listened intently.

After a full minute of silence, Eric said softly, "I don't hear anything."

"I don't think we're being followed," Adam whispered.

"Really?" Jerry said hopefully.

"Let's wait a bit," Sanchez suggested. "Just in case."

They listened for another couple of minutes, though the teens would have guessed it was much longer. Finally, Adam stood. "Come on. Let's go!"

"Just a minute, amigo," Eric said. "It's your turn."

"What?"

"You can be Jerry's crutch for a while."

"Dammit, all right," Adam groused. "But you have to carry these rifles!"

"Give 'em here."

Landa painfully stood with Adam's help. Gonzalez manned the flashlight as they backtracked down the canyon. They were soon back to the split and headed in the direction they should have taken the first time.

Positive they were no longer in danger, they decided they could converse in regular voices. After progressing several yards along their new path, Chulo started growling.

"What is it, boy?" his master asked.

All four stopped. After a long moment, Adam said, "I'll bet it's a coyote."

In response to his words, a rock weighing fifty pounds came crashing down at their feet.

"What the hell?" Sanchez yelled. He jumped backwards, causing Landa to fall.

Chulo barked furiously at the darkness.

"Where did that come from?" Eric sounded scared.

"I don't know!" Adam admitted.

Another rock as big as the first crashed down. It bounced once, then slammed against Eric's leg, knocking him down.

Chulo's barking was more focused. Something was in the canyon in the direction they were heading.

Eric recovered enough to point his flashlight in that direction. Something moved in the dim light. He couldn't hold both his rifle and the light.

Still sitting, he removed Adam's rifle from his shoulder and set down the flashlight. He pulled his own carbine to a firing position and pulled the trigger. Chambering four shells in quick succession, he shot each round at a different spot, fanning out the bullets.

After the fourth shot, something in the canyon snarled in defiance.

"Did you get him?" Adam asked anxiously.

"I don't know!"

They waited for another rock to fly. Nothing came.

"You need to check it and make sure that thing's dead," Jerry insisted.

Eric wasn't so sure that was a good idea. If he only wounded the creature, it could be even more dangerous. He checked his leg where the small boulder hit him. He was bruised. He also had a growing knot on his shin, but he was confident he could still walk.

"Help me up!" He extended his hand.

Adam pulled Eric to his feet, then picked up the flashlight and his rifle. "You want to help me look?"

"I suppose."

"Be careful!" Jerry said, trying to sound encouraging.

Chapter Thirty-Seven

Jerry Landa sat holding Chulo by the collar, restraining him while the other two walked up the canyon. The dog never stopped barking no matter how hard his owner tried to quiet him.

Despite all the yapping behind them, Eric and Adam spoke in whispers. Both had flashlights and their carbines cradled in the crook of their arms, ready to be fired if necessary.

They walked slowly, sweeping their beams, unsure how far they needed to go. Gonzalez guided them along the path of his last shot.

After several yards, Eric stopped. "I think this is far enough."

"Maybe you scared it off." Sanchez pointed his beam further down the canyon. "It got ahead of us when we went up that blind canyon."

"And it's still ahead of us," Gonzalez said, standing. "It's out there . . . somewhere in the darkness."

He looked in the direction of the barking dog. "Jerry's what? A hundred feet away?"

"About that."

"So, whatever's out there threw those rocks a hundred feet. The one that hit me had to be at least fifty pounds. That thing is big!" He shined his light at Adam. "If I hit it, it's gotta be pissed."

"Just a little."

"We need to go back the way we came."

"Why?"

"That thing is sitting out there waiting for us to go up the canyon. As far as I'm concerned, it can wait there for the next month. We need to find our original trail. Head up to the top of the mesa and keep going till we get home."

"What about Jerry?"

"We'll drag him along with us. We don't have a choice."

"He can barely walk on flat ground!"

"We'll figure it out."

It became a long night.

Eric and Adam traded places helping Jerry.

Whoever wasn't supporting their friend had to lug the three rifles. Each weapon had a carrying strap which helped, but they were cumbersome. However, there was one major advantage to being the weapons bearer. You didn't have to listen to Jerry constantly complaining.

Chulo made retracing their original trail easy. He simply followed the scents they left just hours earlier. What slowed them down was Jerry. That extra burden wore out all of them.

During their constant rests they listened for any indication they were being followed. They were sure Chulo would sound the alarm if anything got close. He had better hearing and better smell than any of them.

Daylight was breaking as they descended the slope of Little Creek Canyon. It was familiar territory. The boys knew exactly where they were . . . a mile and a half south of the Gonzalez farm.

After a few minutes of rest, Eric stood. "Okay, hombres. Let's go!"

Landa shook his head. "I can't take another step." His ankle had swollen to the size of a melon. They had tried a splint, but Jerry found it too painful.

"What do you mean? We're almost home!"

"I'm with Jerry," Sanchez said, rubbing his knee. "I think I broke something on the last fall."

"So, you're just going to sit here? What am I supposed to do? Go get someone to carry you home?"

"I don't have a problem with that," Adam admitted.

"Me neither," Jerry agreed.

"You two are worthless!" He shook his head. "How about I sit down, and we all wait till somebody comes looking for us?"

"Sounds like a plan," Sanchez agreed. "What do you think, Jerry?"

"I think it would be better if he found us some water."

"Crap." Eric removed his partners' rifles from his shoulder and tossed them to their owners. "You can carry your own guns, then." He turned and started walking north toward home.

No one noticed Chulo watching the slope they had just descended. His stare was intense and focused.

"What a couple of wusses!" Gonzalez mumbled as he made his way up the canyon.

The floor was strewn with uneven stones. The teen was careful not to aggravate his sore leg. Though he usually took showers, the thought of sitting in a tub of hot water to relieve his pain seemed like a great idea.

It was twenty minutes after he left his companions that Eric heard the rifle reports. They echoed up the canyon from the south. Two rifles were being fired simultaneously.

After several shots, the carbines fell silent.

Gonzalez was torn. He was closer to his farm than to his friends.

If something had happened to Adam and Jerry, his one gun wouldn't make a difference.

He picked up his pace. Help was only minutes away.

Chapter Thirty-Eight

"Dispatch, Patrol One," Lansing said into his mic. "I'm back in my unit."

The sheriff had just finished writing a speeding ticket ten miles south of Las Palmas. His plan was to continue north to Cohino then west toward Dulce.

"Dispatch copies," Sid Barns replied. "Sheriff, I just got a call from a farmer down on *Cañones Creek*. His son and a couple of his friends got attacked in the woods last night."

"Attacked by what?"

"Evidently, they don't know. Do you want to take the call, or should I pass it on to Deputy Redwine?"

"Where's he patrolling?"

"West of the Jicarilla Reservation."

"I'll take it. I'm a lot closer than he is. Which farm am I looking for?"

"Mr. Gonzalez said take County Road 194 to the very end of the road. He'll be the last farm."

"Gonzalez you said?" Lansing jotted the name down in his note pad.

"Yes, sir. Esteban Gonzalez."

"Got it! Patrol One, out."

Heading south on Highway 15, Lansing passed the turnoff to his ranch. He didn't bother to stop. Tina and Marta Gomez were probably in Santa Fe already. The summer tourist season would start in a couple of weeks. The two teachers wanted to hit the boutiques before the retailers jacked up the prices for out-of-state visitors.

Artiga Reservoir came into view as soon as he passed O'Keefe Ranch. The smoke looming over Segovia began showing at the same time. The grey-white billowing column didn't look any better that morning than any other day.

After ten days the Cerro Grande Fire refused to surrender to the human effort to extinguish it. The only victory was most of the town of Los Alamos had been saved as well as the National Laboratory. White Rock had been spared so far. But the deep canyons east and north of Los Alamos were gradually being consumed. Flames had encroached upon the Santa Clara Pueblo lands and would soon spill into San Phillipe County.

Lansing forced the feeling of helplessness from his mind. He kept the promise he made to himself and lit a votive candle when he prayed for the firefighters on the line. He reassured himself that it must have worked. No fatalities had been reported.

He turned onto Highway 296. The road steadily climbed higher until it crossed over the reservoir dam. Two miles past the dam he turned south onto CR 194.

It was a slow, six-mile drive through the canyon. The steep sides of the hills gave way to broad patches of green farmland. Cattle and sheep grazed in open fields. Brown plowed furrows were beginning to green with early summer crops.

The road noticeably ascended as it wound its way higher into the mountains. Lansing thought it was a beautiful drive. He tried to remember the last time he had been there . . . or if he had ever been that way before. With a county of nearly 5,900 square miles and thousands of miles of back roads, it was possible he'd never been there.

Three miles in, he reached the tiny town of Polvadera. Three dozen homes were scattered along a few streets and next to the green fields near the creek. He drove past one small, boarded up building that once had been a store of some sort. The blacktop ended at San Miguel Church. The road, however, continued south.

Gravel pelted the underside of his Jeep as he passed a half dozen houses. Three of the homes appeared to be operational farms.

A farmhouse, barn and several outbuildings marked the end of the dirt road.

Lansing parked next to a truck. After letting dispatch know he would be away from his radio, he got out. A moment later, he was knocking on the front door.

When it opened, he said, "Sheriff Cliff Lansing, ma'am"

"Oh, Sheriff!" the woman exclaimed. "We didn't expect you so soon!"

She opened the door wider. "Please, come in."

He removed his cattleman's hat as he stepped inside.

"I'm Dorothy Gonzalez."

A four-year-old girl peeked out from behind her mother. Lansing smiled at her and nodded.

"Pleased to meet you. Your husband called about some boys being attacked."

"Esteban is with two other fathers . . . They're trying to locate their sons."

"Were these boys hurt in the attack?"

Dorothy fought back tears. "Yes, but we don't know how bad."

Chapter Thirty-Nine

Lansing was confused. "I don't understand. Your husband said these boys were attacked. How could he know that if he doesn't know where they are?"

"My son came home to get help. It's his friends we don't know about."

"So, your son wasn't attacked?"

"No . . . he was," she said, sounding frustrated. "He's in his room getting dressed. He can explain things better than I can."

Dorothy turned to the child next to her. "Edie, go get your brother. Tell him the sheriff needs to talk to him."

"Okay." Edie ran toward the back of the house, yelling, "Eric, the sheriff's here! But you're not in trouble. He just wants to see you!"

Mrs. Gonzalez smiled sheepishly. "Would you care for some coffee?"

"Sounds good."

Lansing sat at the kitchen table. Dorothy set a mug of coffee in front of him.

"Milk and sugar?"

"Just milk."

"It's goat milk. Is that all right?"

"That's fine." Over the years, Lansing never noticed a big difference between the taste of cow milk and goat milk. Goat's milk was not rich in fat, so it resembled bovine skim milk.

As the sheriff took a sip from his mug, a young man appeared in the doorway. His hair looked damp, his clothes fresh and clean.

"Mom, is dad back, yet?" The boy sounded anxious.

"No, *mijo*, not yet." She turned to their guest. "Sheriff, this is my son, Eric."

In his mind, Lansing had conjured up the image of terrified pre-teens, lost in the woods, attacked by a bear or a mountain lion. The "boy" standing in front of him was almost an adult.

He stepped into the room and extended his hand. "Nice to meet you, Sheriff Lansing."

Lansing stood. "Same here." Again, he was taken off guard. Eric's hand was smaller than the sheriff's, but his grip was firm. He wasn't anything close to the child Lansing anticipated.

"Eric, would you like some coffee?"

"Yes, Momma."

The two men took seats at the table. As Eric was being served, Lansing took a note pad from his breast pocket.

"How old are you, Eric?"

"Eighteen." He seemed distracted, constantly glancing from the sheriff to the back door as if expecting it to open at any moment.

"So, you're getting ready to graduate?"

"Next Thursday."

"What about your friends?"

"They're eighteen, too." Gonzalez provided the names of his companions. He also explained his father went with Adam's and Jerry's fathers to help find the boys.

While the teen talked, Lansing noticed the deep concern in his face. He was genuinely worried about his friends.

"Why didn't you go with them?"

"I wanted to. My father told me to stay here and get cleaned up . . . get some rest."

"How bad were your friends hurt?"

Eric's voice quavered. "I-I don't know."

"You weren't with them?"

"Not the last time . . ."

"Not the last time? You mean you were attacked more than once?"

Eric nodded.

"What attacked you?"

The teen cleared his throat. "We don't know." He noticed the questioning look on Lansing's face. "It was dark."

"Was it an animal?"

Eric hesitated. "It could have been. I'm not sure."

"It was a man then . . . or more than one man?"

"I guess it was a man. He threw big rocks at us."

Gonzalez pulled his pants leg up to expose a bruise and large knot on his shin. "One of them bounced and hit me."

Lansing examined the leg. "How did you get away?"

"I fired my rifle at him."

"You had a rifle with you? Why?"

"We were hunting."

Lansing sat back in his seat. "I think we need to start at the beginning."

Before Eric could continue, they heard hollering coming from far away. Lansing, Eric, and Dorothy rushed to the back door.

The fathers were returning. They were coming up the creek but were still hidden by trees along the bank. Eric threw open the door and began running toward the shouts. He had to know what happened to his friends.

Chapter Forty

Tina and Marta Gomez were not expecting the traffic congestion they encountered. It started at the first traffic light they came to in Segovia and continued all the way to Santa Fe. Part of the problem was the entire towns of Los Alamos and White Rock had been evacuated. Half of the populace ended up in Segovia, the other half in Santa Fe.

Five miles south of Segovia was Pojoaque Pueblo. A steady stream of supply trucks crossed under the Highway 15 overpass onto Los Alamos Highway. The six hundred plus wildlands fire fighters had nearly an equal number of support personnel. This small city at the base camp operated on a twenty-four-hour schedule. The workers needed to be fed and watered. Provisions had to be delivered on a steady basis.

Once the trucks were emptied, they had to head south again to Santa Fe or Albuquerque for resupply.

State Police and Santa Fe Sheriff patrol units were everywhere. The teachers counted at least three accidents even though the speed limit seldom got above forty-five miles per hour. Fortunately, none of the accidents appeared life threatening.

Once past Pojoaque the speed limit picked up to sixty-five. A small conciliation since it was less than ten miles to Santa Fe.

Tina was glad Lansing suggested taking his Ford F-150 crew cab for the drive down. She could see the traffic better from that perch. It could also accommodate a lot more purchases than her little Chevy.

Once they were on the streets of the capitol, she found the lumbering pickup problematic, especially in Old Town Santa Fe. The truck was not easy for her to park on the narrow streets. Parallel parking wasn't even a negotiable item.

After figuring out which stores they wanted to visit first, Tina found a centrally located parking lot. Both teachers were in good shape. Hiking a few extra blocks wouldn't bother either one.

Marta Gomez always had a pretty face, but when she started teaching the previous fall, she was overweight. She promised herself she would get rid of the thirty pounds of junk food fat she had acquired as a student. She watched what she ate, established an exercise regimen, and before school was out for the year, she had achieved her goal. She now looked ten years younger. At twenty-four, she could pass for a nineth grader.

The boys who first regarded her as a doughty, chunky schoolmarm of no particular interest were interested now. A couple even asked her opinion of teachers dating students. She made it clear student-teacher relationships were taboo.

The English teacher was grateful when Tina suggested the shopping trip. She needed a completely new wardrobe. She would visit her hometown that Summer. She wanted to look her best just in case she ran into schoolmates who looked down at her years before.

Chapter Forty-One

Ray Cabrera sat at the kitchen table sipping on a mug of coffee, staring at nothing in particular.

Bess glanced at him occasionally while she finished washing dishes. Her husband seemed subdued. It was nearly noon, and he hadn't started on the whiskey. In fact, she was surprised he asked for coffee when he returned from *Lobo Creek Market*.

She knew better than to press him. Ray was not good at expressing much more than anger. If something bothered him, he kept it inside. It would churn and fester until it burst like a boil.

After thirty years, Bess knew the best thing to do was to stand back and try not to get caught in the eruption.

"Would you like some more coffee?" she asked cautiously.

"No," he said vacantly. "No, I don't think so. Thanks anyway."

Bess knew something was going on. Ray Cabrera never said "thanks."

He stood and handed her his cup. His hand trembled. Bess quickly attributed her husband's shakiness to the fact that he hadn't had a drink yet.

"I'm going to check the shed . . . see if we have paint for the *Rancho* sign."

He started toward the front of the house. He had a limp Bess had never seen before.

Ray stopped at the kitchen door.

"I talked to Albert this morning." He made the remark without looking at his wife.

"You did! Where?" Bess braced herself. There had to be more coming.

"At the market . . . He said you two had been talking on the phone."

There it is, Bess thought. *He's getting ready to pounce!* "Yes, we talked."

Ray stood silent for a moment. "Do you talk often?"

"Not as much as I'd like," she answered carefully.

"Maybe you should talk more," he said, finally looking at his wife. "Albert is our son, after all." He paused. "He asked me to tell you hi."

"Oh, he did?"

Ray only nodded, then turned. Grabbing his hat from the wall peg, he continued outside.

Bess was suddenly consumed with questions. *How long did they talk? What did they talk about? Would Ray consider asking their son to dinner? Who the heck was this man she just talked to?*

Chapter Forty-Two

Eric Gonzalez didn't slow down until he reached the group. Lansing was close behind. Neither knew what to expect.

Vernon Sanchez was helping his son. Adam could barely walk. He hadn't broken anything on his fall. However, X-rays would show he dislocated his right kneecap.

Esteban Gonzalez and Martin Landa were both helping Jerry. His broken ankle would need surgery.

"You guys are all right!" Eric exclaimed. "I heard you firing your rifles!"

"Whatever chased us last night was coming down the slope," Adam winced.

"Did you see it?" Eric asked.

"No," Adam admitted. "It was nearly to the creek, though."

"You didn't see anything?" Lansing asked.

"No," Landa admitted, almost in tears. "But we heard . . ." He started choking up. "It killed Chulo!"

Eric stopped, shocked at the news. "Oh, God, no!"

"Sheriff," Esteban said. "Did you hear us yelling? We need an ambulance."

Lansing nodded. "I'll call dispatch from my radio. Are you going to the Gonzalez farm?"

"Yeah," Martin Landa nodded. "These boys need to get stabilized. The less they have to walk, the better."

Lansing returned the nod, then headed immediately for his patrol Jeep.

***

Jerry was sprawled on the sofa, his bare ankle exposed. The sneaker for that foot had been lost hours before. Adam's leg was propped up on an ottoman. Their mothers had been called and now hovered attentively.

Despite their pain, both teens were famished. They had no problem eating the meal Dorothy Gonzalez whipped up.

Lansing wanted to ask questions, but the two sets of parents insisted medical care should come first. Two ambulances were on their way from Segovia.

"Listen," he said to the Sanchez and Landa fathers, "your sons are comfortable. They've eaten something. The paramedics will be here soon. I only want to ask them about what happened up there in Little Creek Canyon.

"Eric Gonzalez can fill me in on the rest."

After a quick discussion with their wives, they gave Lansing the nod.

"What happened up there after Eric left to find help?"

The two teens looked at each other. Adam spoke first.

"I don't know how long Eric had been gone," he began. "Jerry and I were talking when Chulo started growling. He was looking up the slope we had just come down."

"I asked him what he was growling at," Landa added. "He looked at me, then ran into the woods before I could grab him. He was barking like crazy."

"Yeah," Adam continued. "We could hear him. He must have gone a hundred feet in. Suddenly he quit barking. That's when he started snarling, like he was attacking something."

"Chulo was barking and growling," Jerry said. "Then he let out a big yelp. I yelled for him to come back, but I couldn't hear him anymore. That's when I knew he was dead."

"We knew we were next," Adam continued. "We started firing our rifles into the woods. We kept firing till we ran out of bullets."

"We had extra shells in our backpacks," Landa completed. "We reloaded and waited but nothing came out of the woods."

"So, you never saw them?" Lansing asked.

Both teens shook their heads. The sheriff looked at Eric. He shook his head as well.

"You don't know what or who chased you?"

The three continued shaking their heads.

"Then I guess you don't know why then, either."

"No, we don't," Eric said quickly.

Lansing noticed the glances that passed between the three teens. Before he could ask another question, little Edie came running into the room.

"The ambulance people are here!"

"It's about time!" Mrs. Sanchez said.

In the background, the phone rang. A moment later one of the younger Gonzalez boys came in and whispered something to Eric. He hurried out of the room.

General confusion ensued as paramedics came in to assess the status of the teens. Parents tried to talk over each other as they asked questions. Most questions couldn't be answered until after the boys had seen a doctor.

Lansing took control. Everyone except the patients and the medics were ushered out. The parents were assured they would be fully briefed about the status of their sons in due time.

After the assessments were completed, it was decided both teens would be taken to the Presbyterian Hospital in Segovia. The parents expressed concern that the hospital might be saturated with smoke from the Cerro Grande Fire. They were informed the air quality in the hospital was perfectly safe.

Eric, who was busy on the phone, refused any medical attention, insisting he was fine.

The two teens were loaded onto stretchers, then slid into the ambulances. Parents followed in their private vehicles. It wasn't long before the Gonzalez house reached a modicum of normality.

By that time, Lansing had decided what needed to be done next.

Chapter Forty-Three

Lincoln Baca only caught bits and pieces of his sister's conversation. Eric Gonzalez had gotten home after spending the night in the woods. His leg got banged up a little. His two companions were hurt so bad they had to go to the hospital.

The firefighter assumed the boys hurt themselves stumbling around in the dark. If they had asked him, he would have told them to hunker down until daylight. As dry as the forests were, he would have definitely discouraged a campfire.

He nodded to himself how sage his advice was . . . forgetting momentarily he was nursing a broken arm because of his own carelessness in the dark.

The living/dining areas were in one large room. They were only separated by the choice of furniture. Joy came into the dining area. Lincoln had been watching his mother scrape a hummingbird motif onto a pot.

"Mom, can I take the truck?"

Pauline looked up. "Where do you plan on going?"

"I wanted to drive up and see Eric."

"Why?"

"Eric and the other boys were hunting in the forest yesterday . . . tracking a bear. They ran into something else. It chased them all last night. I wanted to make sure he was okay."

"What did they run into?" Lincoln asked, interested.

Joy shook her head. "They don't know . . . They never really saw it."

"Was Eric hurt?" her mother asked.

"Not so much, I don't think. The other two boys are going to the hospital."

"You taking the truck is not a good idea," Pauline said, frowning. "If something happens to your father, or if we have to leave the Pueblo because of the fire, that's our only vehicle. What are the rest of us supposed to do?"

Lincoln would have gladly loaned her his own truck, but it sat next to the house with a broken timing chain. He had no idea when he would have enough money to fix it.

"It's not the end of the world," her mother said, trying to soften her refusal. "You'll see him at school Monday, won't you?"

"Yeah, I guess . . . It's just that I told him I could see him today."

"Well," Pauline sighed, "you'll have to tell him you won't see him today."

Pouting, Joy returned to the living room, picked up the phone and dialed. She listened for a short moment, then slammed the receiver down.

Lincoln had followed her into the living room area. "What's wrong?"

"It's busy!" Joy snapped, flopping down on the sofa.

Lincoln sat in a nearby chair.

"This thing that chased Eric and his friends in the woods . . . they don't know what it was?"

Joy shook her head.

"They don't know why it was chasing them?"

Joy hesitated. "I guess not."

"If they were hunting a bear, they must have had guns. Did they try to shoot at the thing chasing them?"

"I don't know . . . maybe."

"Eric didn't say?"

"Yes." She thought for a second. "He said he fired shots in a canyon, but it was dark. He wasn't sure if he hit anything."

"And it still followed them? How do they know?"

"Jerry Landa's dog ran into the woods this morning. Jerry and Adam Sanchez heard the dog attacking something. The dog let out a huge yelp, then things got quiet. They're sure the dog is dead.

"They fired their rifles into woods. They think they might have killed whatever was chasing them."

"They didn't go look?"

"Jerry can't walk. They think he broke his ankle. Adam tried to go into the woods, but his knee is torn up."

Lincoln sat thinking. Joy tried the Gonzalez number again, but the line was still busy.

"Eric and these other guys . . . they really don't know why they were being chased?"

Joy stared out the window. Eventually, she let out a long, deep breath. "Eric asked me to not say anything . . . but I don't think it matters.

"Yesterday afternoon Adam thought he saw the bear they were hunting. He thinks he shot it. When he did, it let out a scream that scared the crap out of all of them."

"What was it?"

"Like I said, Adam thought it was a bear . . . at first, anyway."

"Did he kill it?"

"They don't know."

"They didn't check?"

"They started to . . . then something started crashing through the trees."

"What?"

"They didn't hang around to find out."

Lincoln leaned back in his chair, lost in his thoughts. He recalled his encounter on Cerro Grande just before his accident . . . his conversation with Uncle Eluterio and the old man's stories about the *atosle*.

He couldn't dismiss the idea that that Eric and his friends crossed paths with the same creatures he had met over a week earlier.

Chapter Forty-Four

Tito Calle found the traffic on Highway 15 to be light for a Saturday afternoon. His guess was it was because of the forest fire southwest of Segovia.

Ten miles north of town he was clear of the smoke. It felt good to breath clean air. He hoped Linda and the boys were experiencing the same thing in Santa Fe.

Once he was on CR 131, he passed a few ranchers out to inspect grazing herds. He found no one on the road as he neared the trees. The scrub desert that passed for grazing pastures gradually transitioned into wooded forest. In the shadow of ten-thousand-foot Cerro Pelon, Calle turned south. He never got a straight answer from Jimmy Clay on how he found the abandoned barn, which wasn't unusual. He never got a straight answer from his former partner about anything.

That wasn't a problem any longer. He found his own buyer for the mag wheels. When that transaction was complete, he would leave the stolen truck at the barn, wipe away any fingerprints, and walk away. He was finished with his life of crime. With Jimmy gone, there was no one to badger him into breaking the law.

Tito didn't concern himself with the fact that he had killed Jimmy Clay. To his mind, that act of murder was totally justified. For starters it was self-defense. Plus, Jimmy was a bully and a wife beater. He was also a thief . . . not to mention a drunk. Calle was positive that if he ever was arrested for the death, no jury would convict him.

"Hell," he thought, "they might even give me a medal."

Calle knew something was wrong before he ever reached the barn. Two of the mag rims lay next to the dirt track leading up to the doors. When he looked up the short hill, the doors of the barn were wide open.

He stopped his pickup short of the building.

Someone had broken into the weather-beaten building. He admitted "broken into" wasn't the correct term to use. There was never a lock on the doors. Jimmy didn't think anyone would look twice at the structure. It appeared like it was about to collapse at any moment.

Tito got out of his truck and cautiously approached. Whoever opened the barn had gotten into the paneled truck. Once again, there was no lock to tamper with.

Three rims were tossed on the ground just outside the truck. Three rims were still in the back. Counting the two next to the road, Calle could account for eight of the twelve rims.

He walked around to the cab. Sunlight shown through a gaping hole in the barn roof. The driver side door was open. Peeking inside, everything else appeared in place.

Climbing behind the wheel, he found the keys over the sun visor. After two tries, the engine started. Maybe the situation wasn't a complete loss after all. The contents of the truck had been scattered only because the perpetrators didn't know their value.

Each of the three sets had a different design. He returned all eight rims to the back of the truck to assess what he had. If he had two complete sets, the drive to Albuquerque would be worth it.

After a quick inspection, he realized he didn't even have one complete set.

"Kids," he thought. "Worthless, punk kids."

Tito started looking in the woods surrounding the barn. After fifteen minutes, he found the first missing rim. He carried it to the barn and threw it into the truck.

"One down, three to go," he thought.

He wandered to the bottom of the hill, checking either side of the track. Two hundred feet from the barn, he decided he was wasting his time. As he was about to return to his truck and cut his losses, his eye caught movement in the trees.

Tito stopped. He studied the shady forest. A dark form darted between tree trunks.

"Hello?" Calle shouted. He took a few steps deeper into the woods.

"I see you!" He waited for a response. "Are you the one who broke into my truck? Did you take my rims?"

A moment later, a missing rim came flying at Calle. If he hadn't jumped out of the way, it would have hit him. Ordinary rims weighed close to thirty pounds. The mag wheels weighed ten pounds less. However, it still took considerable strength to toss one any distance. The mere shape of the rim made gripping it with one hand nearly impossible.

"Bastard!" he shouted. Without thinking, he plunged into the forest to confront his assailant.

Tito could hear him as he ran through the trees. Every once in a while, he caught sight of the dark figure eluding him. That urged him onward, deeper into the forest . . . unaware of what waited for him.

Chapter Forty-Five

"Esteban, what do you think was chasing those boys last night?" Lansing asked after the ambulances left. The two men stood in the yard, talking in hushed tones.

"I don't know, Sheriff," the farmer admitted. "I don't know of anything that can throw rocks like Eric talked about."

"I do," Lansing said definitively. "Another human being."

"You think some person was chasing them?"

"When I asked them why they thought they were being chased, they all glanced at each other before insisting they didn't know. I think they saw something they weren't supposed to. Whoever it was came after them to keep them quiet."

"Damn," Gonzalez swore. "Do you think they'll come after them again?"

"I'm afraid they might."

"What can we do?"

"You need to protect your family. I'll get a deputy up here if you want."

"One deputy won't be able to protect all three families. I'm sure we can take care of our own . . . What are you going to do?"

"I'm going after the man who chased them."

"By yourself?"

"No way . . . but I don't want to drag the State Police into this if it turns out to be nothing. That fire has resources stretched pretty thin. I know some professional hunting guides. They operate the Red Ranch Outfitters out of Lobo Creek. I'll hire a couple of them to help."

"A posse?"

Lansing smiled. "Yeah . . . a posse. With this up and down terrain I don't think horses will work, though. We'll have to hike."

"When will this happen?"

"As soon as I can get them up here." Lansing shielded his eyes as he looked up at the sun. "It's barely noon. We'll have a good six or seven hours of daylight."

"Is there anything me or my wife can do?"

"It would help if you could take us up Little Creek Canyon to where you found those two boys. That will give the trackers a good jumping off point for heading into the woods."

"That won't be a problem. Anything else?"

"Maybe Mrs. Gonzalez can throw together a few sandwiches for us."

"She would be glad to."

Lansing pulled out his cell phone, then held it up for better reception. "I'll need to use your home phone to call the outfitters."

"I'll show you where it is."

The two men went inside. Three of the four Gonzalez children were watching television. Eric was nowhere to be seen.

"I'll have the trackers bring their topographic maps," Lansing said. "I'll need your son to show us where he went."

Esteban nodded. "Edie, go tell Eric the sheriff would like to talk to him again."

"No rush," Lansing said, picking up the phone directory. "It may be an hour before anyone gets here."

Thumbing through the pages, he found the number he wanted.

"*Red Ranch Outfitters.*"

"Hello, this is Sheriff Lansing, San Phillipe County. Who am I talk-ing to?"

"*This is Albert Cabrera, Sheriff. How can I help you?*"

"I need a couple of guides."

"*When?*"

"Today. Some boys were attacked in the woods last night. I need to find this guy before he hurts someone."

Lansing outlined the situation. He didn't have the manpower to conduct a large manhunt. He was confident, though, professional hunting guides could accomplish what he needed. They would be deputized and earn a per diam for their efforts. They would also need to be armed, just in case.

Cabrera explained he was the only Red Ranch guide available. However, he did know of another hunting guide that might be interested.

The sheriff provided directions. The guide assured him they would be there within an hour.

Chapter Forty-Six

It took Linda Calle thirty minutes to convince her sister-in-law they should take their boys to Santa Fe. The trip would be Linda's treat. She would pay for lunch, the movie tickets, even the gas. The boys would have a great time plus they would be away from the smoke for a few hours.

Ramona's only reason for hesitation was that she didn't want to be away if Jimmy came home. It wasn't that she missed him. He would expect her to be there when he returned. She feared he would beat her when she got back.

"Ramona," Linda scolded, "when was the last time you saw him?"

"Tuesday."

"You said you called the police and the hospitals. No one's seen him. Do you really think he'll show up today?"

"No . . . I don't know," she whined.

"He's been gone for four days. Have you filed a missing-persons report with the police?"

"No," she admitted.

"That's because you don't want him to come home, do you?"

Ramona hesitated. "I-I guess not."

"Then there's no reason why we can't drive over to Santa Fe today."

"Okay," she finally agreed. "You're right. Jimmy Junior and I will be over in fifteen minutes."

***

Neither mother understood why the four-lane highway between Segovia and Santa Fe was so busy. It didn't dawn on them the displaced families from Los Alamos or White Rock were looking for the same kind of escape as they were. Plus, they didn't tie-in the heavy truck traffic with the Cerro Grande firefighters.

Once they were in the capitol, they looked for a place to purchase a newspaper. It would have showtimes for the movies playing at the *Cinema 6*. They made a quick stop at a *Shell Gas Food Mart* for a copy of the *Santa Fe New Mexican*, then headed for the closest *McDonald's*.

The three boys, Juan, Roberto and Jimmy Junior, were disappointed that *Viva Rock Vegas* wasn't playing any longer. However, they were overjoyed that *Disney's Dinosaur* had started that weekend. Linda insisted they get there early just in case there were crowds.

It turned out she was more correct than she anticipated. The 1:50 showing was already sold out. Tickets were available for the 3:40 screening, but they were still advised to get in line early. The boys had to be bought off with ice cream.

They wouldn't be heading home until after 5:00. Linda and Ramona hoped their kids would be exhausted by then and sleep once they were back in the car.

Chapter Forty-Seven

Tina Morales had parked in the municipal lot on East Water Street. The choice served two purposes. First, there were over a dozen places to shop within a two-block area. It would be easy to secure purchases inside the truck before exploring other establishments.

Second, the lot was just around the corner from *Saint Benedict's Rialto*. Tina tried to visit Roger and Eileen Porter whenever she visited Santa Fe. They had met two years earlier at *Saint Anthony's Monastery in the Canyon*. They were now dear friends and Tina wanted Marta to meet them.

The shopping was more arduous than Tina anticipated. Marta Gomez was five sizes smaller. As a result, she had to try on every garment to make sure it fit. By noon, they had visited only half of the available shops.

That's when Tina announced she was hungry. They finally found a Mexican restaurant they could both agree on. They also agreed it felt good to sit and rest.

Halfway through the meal Tina's cell phone rang. It was a number she didn't recognize. She gave Marta a questioning look when she answered. "Hello?"

"Tina, it's Cliff."

"Oh, hi, Sweetie! Where are you calling from?"

"I'm at a farm up in the mountains. I couldn't get any reception on my cell so I'm using a landline."

"Ah, I see. Marta and I were just finishing lunch."

"Have you cleaned out all the shops in Santa Fe?"

"Not yet," she laughed. "We still need a couple of more hours."

"Listen, Hon, I wanted you to know I might not be home tonight."

"Why? What's going on?"

Lansing explained the situation. He and two hunting guides were heading into the Jemez Mountains. They needed to find the person or persons who chased and attacked three teens. Two of the boys were in the hospital. A dog was killed. He needed to stop things before they escalated.

"Isn't it a bit late to start any search?"

"If we wait any longer, the trail will just get colder."

"You know I worry about you."

"Yes, I do. That's why I'm calling. I'll be heading out as soon as the guides get here."

"Well," she said, reluctant to hang up. "You be careful . . . You have a jacket, don't you?"

"Yes, I do, Miss Morales."

She blushed at being mocked. "That will be enough, Lansing. You know I love you."

"I love you, too. I'll call as soon as we wrap things up."

"You'd better . . . and I don't care if it's three in the morning. You call me."

"I will. G'bye."

"Bye-bye, Cliff." Tina pushed the red "End Call" button on her phone.

"What's going on?" Marta asked as she took a sip of her tortilla soup.

"Oh, my sheriff is off chasing bad guys in the woods."

"What happened?"

"Some teens were attacked . . . yesterday, I guess."

"They weren't any of our students, were they?"

"I don't know . . . He didn't say. But two of the boys are in the hospital."

"Wow! Were they badly hurt?"

The chemistry teacher shrugged. "Bad enough to end up in the hospital."

Tina poked at her food. Suddenly she wasn't very hungry.

"Are you ready to hit some more shops?" she asked.

Marta wiped her mouth and nodded. "Yes. We can keep going as long as my money lasts."

Tina signaled the waitress for their bill.

Chapter Forty-Eight

Albert found Ray Cabrera right where his mother said he would be, putting fresh paint on the *Rancho Cazador* sign. The younger Cabrera brought his Expedition to a stop and got out.

"Hey, Ray!" he called.

Cabrera stopped his brush in mid stroke and turned, unaware that anyone was near.

"Albert, twice in one day! What are you doing here?"

Albert was taken off guard. His father actually sounded like he was glad to see him. "I got a call from the sheriff. He needs a couple of trackers. I was wondering if you were interested."

"Why ask me? What's wrong with your partners?"

"They're off doing other things.

"When Sheriff Lansing asked for two guides, I immediately thought of you. Sounds like we'll have to hoof it through some rough terrain, though." He paused. "That is, if your leg isn't too bad."

"Ah, my leg's fine. A long walk is probably the best thing for it." He set his brush on the rim of the paint can. "When does the sheriff want us?"

"I'm headed there now. Your place was on the way. That's why I stopped."

Ray nodded. "What are we supposedly tracking?"

"Someone attacked three boys in the mountains last night. Put two of them in the hospital. We're going after whoever did it."

"A manhunt, huh?" Ray stared into the distance. "Been a while since I did anything like that."

"The sheriff said he'll pay us. I don't know how much."

"I don't think the money matters." Cabrera picked up his paint and brush. "Albert, can you run me up to the house? I need to throw this stuff in the shed. Let your mother know what's going on."

"Sure, Ray." He almost said "Dad." He didn't because he wasn't ready. There were too many years of anger and hurt to overcome before that could happen.

***

Bess Cabrera was thrilled to see her husband and son about to do something together. At first, she thought Albert's offer was made because she had asked him to. While Ray changed into hunting attire, her son assured her he actually needed his father's help.

Both were surprised at how readily Ray accepted the job.

"I noticed he hasn't started drinking yet," Albert observed. "I'm sure he restocked his supply this morning."

"When?" Bess asked.

"He had a bag when he walked out of the Lobo market."

"He went to the store for me. I wanted to do some baking."

"So, he didn't get whiskey?"

Bess shook her head.

"Is something wrong with Ray?"

Bess knitted her brow. "I don't think so."

She knew that was an untruth. She had been thinking something was wrong all morning. It was past noon, and her husband hadn't taken a drink all day. She couldn't remember the last time that happened.

Until that day, even mentioning Albert's name was taboo. Ray considered his son disloyal. He had betrayed him and left with his two best hunting guides. If *Rancho Cazador* ever failed, it would be Albert's fault.

Now, father and son had been enlisted by the county sheriff to do some tracking. Ray was acting as if nothing was ever wrong between the two.

"Your father's fine," she insisted. "He's just turning over a new leaf. That's all."

Chapter Forty-Nine

Both men reassured Bess they would be careful as they kissed her goodbye.

She stood in the front door and waved as she watched Albert's Expedition disappear down the road. Once they were gone, she immediately looked up the number she wanted.

Ed Stevenson answered. *"Hello?"*

"Ed, this is Bess Cabrera."

"Oh, hi, Bess. How are you?"

"I'm fine. I'm fine. I needed to ask you a question."

"Sure."

"Did anything happen yesterday?"

"What do you mean?"

"When you and Ray were driving those cattle . . . did something happen to Ray?"

"Oh, that! Yeah, he kinda got thrown off his horse."

"How? Was he drunk?"

"No . . . well, I don't know. He mighta been. He smelled like he had a few. But we were heading home after we got the herd to pasture. Ray's horse got spooked by a rattle snake and reared up on him. Ray fell off . . . guess he hit his head."

"Oh, my God! How bad was he hurt?"

"He got knocked out. I guess he musta been unconscious for about five minutes. At first, I thought he was dead. Wally, my foreman, made sure he was still breathing. About the time I was getting ready to call an ambulance, he came to. I told him he needed to see a doctor, but he said was all right."

"Did he seem like he was all right?"

"Oh, I don't know. He was a bit unsteady getting back in the saddle. But he seemed okay by the time he got back to the horse trailer. Why? Is something wrong with him?"

"I'm not sure . . . He's just acting different."

"What does that mean . . . he's acting different?"

Bess described how "pleasant" Ray had been all day. She told Stevenson how nice he had been to Albert . . . How the two of them were working together. On top of everything else, he hadn't had a drink all day.

"That is different! Plus, I don't think I've ever heard Ray say anything good about that boy of yours."

"Yes, I know. Maybe I can get him in to see the doctor on Monday."

"You sure you want to do that? Sounds like that fall knocked some sense into him."

Bess laughed. "You might be right. Maybe I should leave well enough alone."

"If there's anything I can do, Bess, let me know."

"Thanks, Ed. I will."

Bess hung up the phone and thought about the conversation. Ray fell from his horse and got knocked out. Could a bump on the head cause a radical change in someone's personality? And if it could, would it last?

Chapter Fifty

Joy walked into the dining room after hanging up the phone.

"Is Eric disappointed he won't see you today?" her brother asked.

"Maybe a little," she said, frowning. "He said he's been up for two straight nights. All he wants to do now is sleep."

Lincoln tried to raise his arm to lessen the strain on his neck. He got little relief though because the arm was anchored against his body. Laying down usually helped. He stood to go to his room.

"The sheriff's up there at Eric's farm," Joy said as an afterthought. "He hired a couple of hunting guides."

Lincoln stopped. "Hunting guides? For what?"

"The sheriff thinks the boys were attacked by a man."

"Why a man?"

"He said only a human could throw rocks the way Eric described. They want to track this guy down before he hurts anyone else."

"They can't do that!" Lincoln blurted out.

"Why not?" his mother asked, looking up from her pottery work. She had been listening to her children's conversations all morning.

Lincoln sat down. He had hoped what he had encountered on Cerro Grande . . . what he talked about with Uncle Eluterio . . . could remain a secret. He personally felt guilty for starting the fire that drove the *atosle* from their home.

The more he thought about Eric's experience in the woods the night before, the more he was convinced the teens were chased by an *atosle*. It was possible they had killed one of the creatures he saw ten days earlier. That's why they were attacked.

Now the sheriff and two hunters were going to track down the brute. If they were successful, they might even kill it. Lincoln couldn't have that death on his conscience.

"What's wrong?" his sister asked.

Lincoln had spent long nights thinking on how he would describe his Cerro Grande encounter, if he was ever asked. He told his story. Then he continued with what Uncle Eluterio discussed. Finally, he tied Eric's attack to what he knew about the *atosle*.

"You need to call your boyfriend back," Lincoln pushed. "He needs to stop the sheriff."

"You have to tell Eric why," Joy said. "And you'll have to tell the sheriff."

Lincoln nodded. "I'll do that . . . but you have to call Eric now!"

Joy got back on the phone. Mrs. Gonzalez answered. Eric wasn't available. He was asleep.

The sheriff wasn't available either. Mr. Gonzalez was taking him and two hunting guides into the woods to track the boys' assailant. They had already been gone for fifteen minutes.

Dorothy Gonzalez insisted there was no way she could contact them.

Joy looked at her brother and shrugged helplessly.

"I have to stop them," Lincoln insisted. He looked at his mother. "I really need the truck."

"No," Pauline said flatly. "For the same reasons I gave your sister. Besides, you can't drive. Not in your condition. And you certainly can't go tromping through the woods."

Lincoln looked at his sister. "Would you come with me?"

"Sure," Joy said. "But how are we going to get there?"

"Leave that to me."

Chapter Fifty-One

Cliff Lansing stepped outside when he saw the Ford Explorer pull up, surprised Albert Cabrera arrived as quickly as he had. He was less than thrilled when he saw who Albert brought with him. The sheriff had known Ray Cabrera for twenty years. He couldn't remember ever having a single, pleasant encounter with the man.

The old hunting guide usually reeked of whiskey. He constantly fought with county, state and federal officials over the proper hunting permits for his out-of-state clients. He was often cited for trespassing on private lands. The courthouse clerks shuddered when he approached their desks. The sheriff's office was constantly called to drag him away after he ranted and railed against supposedly unfair taxes or fees.

"Afternoon, Sheriff," Albert said.

"Hi, Albert." He nodded toward the guides. "Hello, Ray."

The elder Cabrera returned the nod. "Sheriff."

"Did you bring those maps?"

"I sure did," Albert said, retrieving a folder from the rear seat.

"Let's go inside. Eric Gonzalez needs to give us an idea of where he and the other boys were attacked."

***

Albert looked through his folder's content, finding the maps he wanted. He spread three contour maps on the table. The maps were sixteen inches wide by twenty-four inches high. Four inches represented one mile. Contours were spaced at twenty-foot intervals with hundred-foot contours slightly darker. Streams, even if they were intermittent, were thin, blue lines. Paved roads were parallel solid lines, unpaved were parallel dashed lines, trails, single dashed lines.

Lansing, Esteban and Eric had joined the hunting guides at the table. They were amazed at the detail on each map.

"I'm not sure where you went," Albert said to Eric. He pointed at the northernmost point on the center map. "Here's Polvadera." He traced his finger to the south eight inches. "This marks the end of County Road 194. The black squares are your house and out-buildings.

"Do you think you went more than four miles south of here?"

"No," Eric shook his head. "We were about two miles south of the farm."

Esteban pointed at a separate canyon six inches south and east of his farm. "There, in Little Creek Canyon. That's where we found the Landa and Sanchez boys."

"Did you come from east or west of that point?"

"We came from the east." The teen leaned forward for a closer look. He traced his finger as far east as he could on the center map, then transitioned to the next.

"This little canyon." He tapped on a spot four inches from the edge. "We went up that way but had to turn around."

He dropped his finger to the south an inch. "I think this is where we went to the top of the ridge. There's a clearing. That's as far east as we went."

"That's where you saw the men?" Lansing asked.

Eric hesitated. "We didn't really see anyone."

"But they started chasing you . . . right?"

Eric nodded. "Yeah, I guess so."

"How did you know they were coming after you?"

"We heard them."

"Did they shoot at you?"

"No."

"Were they yelling?"

"Yes," Eric agreed, ". . . plus we could hear them coming through the forest at us."

"It scared you?"

"Oh, hell yeah!"

"Eric," his father growled. "Watch your language!"

"Yes, sir."

Ray Cabrera pointed at a dirt road running down the eastern edge of the second map. "What road is that?"

Albert leaned in for a better look. "That's County Road 131."

"That comes south out of Artiga," Lansing added.

"Another road branches off and goes south of Cerro Pelon," Cabrera observed. "If we're trying to hunt this man down, wouldn't it be faster if we drove that route, then hiked west?"

"That's true," the sheriff agreed. "But the other two boys think they might have shot the guy. He could still be there in Little Creek Canyon . . . dead. Or he might have collapsed getting away. That's why I'm bringing you two along, to follow his trail."

Ray nodded. "Makes sense."

Lansing was struck by two things. Cabrera didn't reek of alcohol, and he wasn't his typically argumentative self.

"Okay, then," the sheriff said. "We need to get moving while there's daylight.

"Esteban, you ready?"

"Sure." He handed Lansing the sandwiches Dorothy made.

Lansing divided them with the Cabreras.

"Isn't the boy coming with us?" Ray asked.

"My son's been up for most of two nights," Gonzalez said. "He needs rest. The sheriff said he didn't have to go."

"We'll be fine, Ray."

"Why's the dad coming?"

"He's going to show us where he found the other kids. We'll start our search from there."

Cabrera shrugged. "You're the boss."

Chapter Fifty-Two

"You sure this is the spot?" Ray Cabrera asked, looking further down the canyon.

"Yes," Esteban said firmly. "Look around. You'll see the shell casings from the boys' rifles."

Lansing looked at the steep slope. "So, the trail starts over there?"

"Yeah." Gonzalez pointed at a large rock. "That's where Dan Landa went in the woods. He was trying to find their dog, but I don't know how far up the slope he went."

"Did he find anything?" Albert asked.

"No, not that I know of."

"Thanks a lot for your help, Esteban," the sheriff said. "We'll take it from here."

As Gonzalez turned to go home, Lansing gestured toward the forest. "One of you need to take the lead."

"I'll go, Ray," Albert said. "You can back me up."

Ray shrugged. "Whatever you want."

Lansing was caught off guard by Albert calling his father by his first name. He was equally confused by Ray's subdued demeanor. This didn't seem to be the same man he had disliked for two decades.

Albert could easily see where the three teens made a trail. Pine needles and leaves on the ground had been disturbed where Jerry Landa was being supported by Eric. Adam Sanchez had scraped a path where he dragged his bad leg.

At least along this portion, the trail was so easy to follow Lansing felt he could have done the search himself. He said nothing, though. Along with their tracking expertise, both Cabreras brought rifles.

Lansing carried one himself. He hoped that kind of fire power wouldn't be necessary, but he preferred having too much than too little.

Fifty yards in, Albert stopped. There was a large area where needles and leaves had been disturbed. "Something went on here."

"The Landa's dog attacked whoever followed them," Lansing said. "The boys in the canyon heard the dog yelp in pain, then it went silent. That's when they fired their rifles."

Albert knelt for a closer inspection. He picked something up. "Here's a tuft of short, tan fur."

"The dog was a German Shepherd."

The guide nodded. "This looks like it could be from a German Shepherd."

"There's some blood over here," Ray said, pointing to a spot on the ground. "Not a lot, though."

The other two came over for a closer look.

"Could be from the dog," Lansing observed. "Or those boys might have hit the guy following them." He looked around. "I don't see the dog's body anywhere."

"Must have crawled off to die," Ray said. "That's my guess."

The sheriff thought collecting a sample of the blood would be wise, forensically speaking. He wasn't equipped for that. Besides, he wasn't there to collect evidence. He was looking for a man . . . one that might have been shot.

"Let's keep going," he directed. "I'd like to wrap things up before dark."

"Sure," Albert said, nodding. He immediately picked up the trail again. Ray followed several feet behind, examining either side of the path, looking for clues as to who they might be chasing.

Lansing brought up the rear. It was an unfamiliar place for him. He was used to taking point on any operation. He knew he would assume that role if they ran into trouble.

Chapter Fifty-Three

Marta Gomez turned sideways to look at her profile in the mirror.

"Tina, I can't find any jeans that will fit," she huffed. "You'd think there would be at least one woman's boutique that had something. We've been to at least a dozen. No one has anything my size."

"You know why?" Tina asked.

"Why?"

"Because you're looking at adult jeans. You've lost so much weight you need to look at a junior size."

"I thought about that . . . I don't think any of these stores carry junior miss jeans."

"I suggest we go to *J.C. Penny's*. They usually have a good selection."

"Is there one around here?"

"There's a *Penny's* in the Santa Fe Place Mall."

"Is that very far?"

"Three miles, maybe."

"You don't mind going there?"

"Not really. I wouldn't mind looking around myself."

It was midafternoon. The sun wouldn't set till after 8:00. Besides, Tina was in no hurry. The ranch house would be empty, and she had no idea when Cliff would be getting home.

"Let me change and we can go."

Tina Morales considered the trip a success. She had found everything she wanted.

Marta had been more selective on what she spent her money on. If she saw something she liked, she checked the price before trying it on.

The tourist season markups hadn't started yet, but Santa Fe boutique shopping was never going to be cheap.

There was a time when Tina protected her money the same way. Not having to spend her salary on food and rent left her more disposable income.

"You know," Tina said as they walked back to the parking lot. "I'm having a lot more fun shopping with you than I ever would with Cliff."

"What's wrong? Doesn't he like to shop?"

"Does any man? He gives lip service to my shopping . . . claims he doesn't mind coming along. But that's a big, fat lie.

"He taps his foot and stares into the distance. It's easy to tell he'd rather be somewhere else. It's even worse getting him to shop for himself. He'd be perfectly happy to wear his uniform seven days a week.

"I try to remind him he won't be a sheriff forever."

"What does he say to that?"

"I might be. You don't know," Tina laughed.

The teachers were frustrated at how much foot traffic they encountered in Old Town Santa Fe. They forgot the capitol city was the most visited tourist attraction in the entire state. Taos ran a close second.

The municipal parking lot was completely full when they reached the pickup. The back seat was crowded with shopping bags, but not to the point of overflowing.

As soon as they were inside, Tina had Marta hand her a Santa Fe city map from the glove compartment.

"What are you looking for?" Gomez asked.

"How to get to Santa Fe Place."

"I thought you knew your way around town."

"I know how to get to the capitol building. It's only a couple of blocks from here. I know how to get to this parking lot. Anyplace else, I need a map."

She located their position. Then she found Santa Fe Place shopping mall.

"I am not a creative driver," Tina admitted. "I'm not going to try and find the quickest way. I tried that last September. All it did was get me in trouble. I ended up lost in the Navajo Badlands and nearly died."

She studied the street names. "The mall is just off Cerrillos Road."

She traced the street to Old Town Santa Fe. "I can take West Alameda to Galisteo Street. That'll run into Cerrillos. That takes us straight to the mall," she said, smiling.

"Do you want me to put the map back?"

"Oh, hell no. We're not at the mall, yet."

Pulling onto the street, Tina had to negotiate traffic from both vehicles and pedestrians. Even after getting onto Cerrillos, the drive was long, with too many lights and too much traffic. Coming from the northeast there was no turn directly into the mall from the divided highway.

Tina missed the turn at the light and had to go down another block before she could make their way back. Their store was at the east end of the mall.

"Will going home be easier?" Marta asked, after they parked. There was a tinge of doubt in the question.

"I don't know, Marta," Tina sighed. "I just don't know."

Chapter Fifty-Four

Tito Calle finally realized he was chasing two individuals. They darted behind trees and hid in shadows too far apart to be a single person. They were also too far ahead for Calle to get a good look. He had no idea how far he had chased them, or for how long. When his quarry went up a slope to the top of a ridge, he decided he'd had enough. It was time to head back to his truck.

Three whoops sounded from above.

He turned in response to the warning, jumping out of the way as another rim sailed through the air at him.

He chased the mag wheel as it bounced into the woods. As he picked it up, he saw a serious dent along the edge. He would never be able to sell anything so damaged.

His anger overruled any reason he had left. Those two thieves had ruined his plans. He was going to pocket a quick thousand dollars, hand the money to his wife and walk away from any more crimes. Now he had nothing to show for his efforts. Someone had to pay.

He touched the knife on his belt to make sure it was still there. He had killed one man that week. Disposing of two more wouldn't bother his conscience at all.

Returning to the bottom of the ridge, he looked up and saw movement.

He started up the slope as quietly as possible. This time he didn't yell or curse. There would be no warning that he was coming. He climbed the four hundred feet to the top of the ridge, but his tormentors were nowhere to be seen.

"So, we are going to play games," he whispered, peering over the descent on the far side. The ground was grass covered with stones scattered about. He kicked at one with his heel, loosening it from the turf. When it was free, he picked it up. It weighed eight pounds he guessed.

Walking back to the edge, he threw the stone into the forested slope as hard as he could.

He couldn't decipher the response. He heard the same whoops as earlier. This time, though they were definitely from two individuals. The whoops were accompanied by a kind of laughter.

The taunting only infuriated Tito more. He sent three more rocks into the forest.

The whoops and laughter continued. He started down the slope with a score to settle.

Chapter Fifty-Five

The Twins were thirteen years old. Nearly as tall as their mother, they had fended for themselves for a year, though they still kept close to their parents. It would be eight more years before they grew as large as their father.

Their kind had a limited oral construct. But like other great apes their language was supplemented by hand movements and facial gestures.

The Twins had one additional dimension to their communications. They could practically read each other's minds, which eliminated the need for a complex vocabulary. By Twin One visualizing what Twin Two thought, they didn't need to name a new object like a shiny, mag wheel. Or develop a term for "throw." They instinctively knew what the other one wanted.

When they did speak to each other, it was in a tongue their parents didn't recognize.

The Twins possessed one more characteristic foreign to their parents. They had a sense of humor . . . a wicked sense of humor. They liked to tease . . . a trait their father failed to appreciate. There were so few of their kind, though, they were forced to inflict their vicious pranks on any unfortunate creature that crossed their paths.

Bears were the most fun. But mountain lions, coyotes, racoons and deer all could fall victim to their mischief. Smaller animals like prairie dogs, rabbits, and squirrels were tormented to death. Since the ultimate goal was a meal, such cruelty was merely a byproduct.

In their younger days, they were warned against exposing themselves to humans. There was a time when their forebearers were hunted nearly to extinction. Men should be avoided at all costs. Blending into their surroundings was a vital skill. Their kind had been so successful with hiding, that humans debated whether or not they even existed.

As the Twins' independence increased, the thought of teasing humans became more tantalizing. Their pranks were always done at night, so it was easy escape into the darkness. Campers in tents were their favorite targets. There was also the occasional remote cabin that attracted their attention. The problem with cabins, though, was that men inside carried metal sticks that made loud noises and spit tiny rocks. The rocks could hurt if they hit you.

They had a new game now. Running across the path of moving metal cabins at night. The cabins were propelled on round things at their base and traveled on wide paths, some of which had hard surfaces. It was fun to see if they could get these cabins to swerve off the paths. Sometimes they would even crash into trees.

They had seen deer and elk play the same game. Once in a while they didn't move quickly enough and were killed by the moving cabins. Sometimes the people inside would put the dead animal on their cabin and leave. If they didn't, the Twins and their parents enjoyed a free meal.

A few nights earlier they played their game of "chicken." They dashed in front of a cabin that made tremendous clanking sounds when it veered off the path, though it didn't crash. The Twins were intrigued. As they watched the little red lights disappear down the path, they both wanted to know what made that wonderful noise.

They followed.

Sometime later another cabin came down the road directly at them. It was smaller than the first. However, they chose not to play their game. They were on a quest.

Finally, the trail led them to a very large, wooden cabin. The doors opened easily. Inside they found the metal, rolling cabin they sought. There were no humans around so they could take their time exploring.

They properly guessed the noisy things they sought were inside the back of the metal cabin. It took little time for them to break into the paneled truck.

Metal round things were strewn around the floor. In the dark, it was impossible to see how shiny the objects were. In the daylight they became even more intrigued with their discovery.

Twin One picked up a wheel and slammed it against the metal wall. That produce the wonderful clang they wanted. Twin Two joined in.

The new game didn't last long though. The reverberation of the loud bang of metal against metal hurt their ears.

They experimented with throwing the wheels against different objects . . . the side of the wooden cabin, the side of the metal cabin, rocks, trees. They finally decided they got the best effect by standing outside and tossing a wheel into the back of the cabin. They got the clang they wanted without hurting their ears.

After a while, they grew tired of the game. It was late and they needed to eat. Despite the fact that they had a wide foraging range, they kept coming back to the round things. They were intriguing and fun to throw, not to mention so very shiny. They did realize their noise making game might attract unwanted visitors, so that came to an end. But the visits didn't.

When they returned that Saturday, they discovered a man messing with the big, metal cabin. He first started the engine, then stacked the wheels in the back. He searched outside the wooden cabin. When he found a wheel, he returned it to his big, metal cabin, throwing it with the others.

The Twins looked at each other. This was unsatisfactory. He was going to take their new, shiny round things away and they couldn't allow that. Their newest game challenged their throwing accuracy. Their targets were trees. They quickly retrieved two of the mag wheels they had callously thrown aside.

They stayed hidden in the woods as they watched the man look for the wheels further and further from the wooden cabin. Twin One stepped from one tree to another.

The man saw the movement. He edged himself toward the woods and began yelling.

The Twins knew they had been spotted. Twin Two stepped from behind his tree and launched his wheel. The missile barely missed the man. It also infuriated him. He began yelling and chasing after them.

That's what they wanted.

The Twins had no problem keeping well ahead of their pursuer. Nearly to the top of a ridge, Twin One let out three whoops, then hurled his wheel at the human. He made the warning to make sure the man moved away in time.

The Twins didn't want to kill him. Not yet anyway. They were having too much fun antagonizing him.

They had no more shiny, round things to throw. But they had other ideas on how to keep the chase going.

Chapter Fifty-Six

"You're going to try to stop the sheriff, so he doesn't shoot who?" Serita Silva asked for the third time.

"These people who live in the forests," Lincoln Baca answered . . . for the third time.

"Are they Tewa, like us?"

Serita was thrilled that Lincoln took her up on the offer to give him a ride. Her shift at the Dollar Store ended at noon so she was available the rest of the day. She was a little less thrilled when he said he needed a ride to a mountain farm twenty miles past Artiga. Her hope for a quiet time with the firefighter was squashed when she found out Joy Baca was coming along.

"No," Joy said from the back seat. "They're not Tewa. They're not Pueblo people . . ."

"They just live alone in the forests," Lincoln completed. "When we started the fire on Cerro Grande, we destroyed their home."

Lincoln was having doubts about calling Serita. The high school senior had made a career of being petite and cute. But even Joy Baca, one of her best friends, admitted the girl was far from bright. Lincoln suspected that was why he had shied away from dating her.

The other issue was her car . . . a ten-year-old Chevy Citation, two-door hatchback. The hood was crumpled. The passenger door had a severe dent. The red paint had faded to resemble the patches of rust. And beyond the appearance, the whole automobile rattled as if it was about to fall apart.

"But I don't understand how you'll find the sheriff."

"Eric Gonzalez knows where the sheriff's going," Joy explained. "We're driving to his farm. He'll show us the way."

Serita glanced at Lincoln. "You're going into the forest like that?"

"What do you mean 'like that?' "

"With a broken arm."

"Why not? I'm not going to walk on my arm."

Serita looked at Joy through the rearview mirror. "You're not going into the woods, too, are you?"

"Of course, I am."

"But why?"

"In case Eric needs help . . . beside I haven't seen him since Wednesday. After graduation, I don't know when I'll see him again."

The driver sat silent for a moment. "I'm coming, too."

"What?" Lincoln exclaimed. "No. That's not a good idea."

"What if you need help, Lincoln? I want to be there in case you need me. Besides, you'll need a ride home when this is over."

"Great," he sighed, looking out the window. "We can stumble around the woods and play *Friday the Thirteenth.*"

"At least we'll know enough to run if we hear any Texas Chainsaws," Joy kidded.

"That's not funny," Serita said sternly.

The Baca siblings looked at each other. The expression on the girl's face told them she truly believed those slasher movies actually took place.

All three agreed it was great to escape from the smoke that enveloped their community. The bright sunlight was a welcome reminder the world might soon return to normal.

There was little highway traffic once they were north of Segovia. The road was familiar to most members of the Pueblo. During the political strife of the nineteen thirties, several families left Santa Clara and moved to Canjilon fifty miles north. Despite the bad feelings between groups, it wasn't a complete break. Blood ties ran deep, and extended families visited each other often.

"We're coming up on Artiga," Lincoln said. "We'll take the turnoff to the reservoir about six miles past the town." He strained to look at the car's gauges. "Are you doing all right on gas?"

Serita checked. "I'll need to fill up before we head home."

"Then let's wait," Lincoln said with a hint of impatience. "We need to catch up to the sheriff."

Chapter Fifty-Seven

The trail Albert Cabrera followed alternated between blatantly obvious to impossible to see. The track disappeared completely over bare ground with little grass to disturb. In those cases, the younger guide zigzagged back and forth looking for his next hint.

The top of the first ridge was forested, but not nearly as much as the climb up. In the breaks between trees, they could see Cerro Pelon jutting up nearly three miles to the east.

The descent into the next canyon was down a treeless slope.

Lansing wasn't completely sure what Ray was doing. He seemed to be examining the ground parallel to his son's track. Sometimes he ranged several yards to either side. Having to wait for him to catch up slowed their progress.

"Exactly what are you doing, Ray?" Lansing finally asked, hoping to speed things along.

"What the hell do you think I'm doing, SHERIFF?" the older man snapped. He spat out Lansing's title as if it was the nastiest word he could summon. "I'm looking for tracks. Those boys could have been chased by more than one man. Right?"

"Yeah, sure," Lansing admitted. He was confused by Cabrera's sudden change in behavior. "What have you found?"

"Nothing." He hurried past the sheriff to catch up with his son. "Albert, do you think we can take a short rest?"

Albert looked at Lansing. "You don't mind stopping, do you? Ray was thrown from a horse yesterday. I think he's hurting a bit."

"No problem." Lansing quickly dismissed Cabrera's sudden surliness as an indication the man was in pain. He looked at the old man. "We'll take as long as you need, Ray."

"All right." Cabrera lowered himself to one knee, using his rifle for support. His son knelt next to him.

Lansing found a tree to lean against a few yards from his guides. The father and son team talked in low tones. Ray occasionally glanced in his direction, but he thought little of it.

The sheriff knew nothing about the Cabrera family dynamics. He had heard rumors that Ray and Albert had a falling out years earlier. That prompted Albert and two other hunting guides to start *Red Ranch Outfitters*. Knowing about Ray's alcohol problems convinced him the younger Cabrera simply got tired of the old man's drunken abuse. Who could blame him?

That day, however, the Cabreras acted as if they were best buddies. Ray Cabrera had obviously changed his ways. Lansing had no other explanation.

The sheriff started their hike wearing his jacket. It wasn't long before he got too hot. Taking it off, it became awkward carrying both a coat and a rifle. Now, standing still, the cool mountain air began to seep in. The sun was racing for the horizon and the canyon floors were dark with shadows. Slipping it on, he was glad for its warmth.

After ten minutes, Albert stood and walked over to Lansing.

"Ray says he's ready to go. If he falls behind, he told me to not worry. He'd catch up."

"If that's all right with you, then let's go."

Ray forced himself to stand, then fell in behind Lansing.

The sheriff hoped their progress would be faster now that they didn't have to wait for the old guide. It also allowed him to watch Albert look for the trail.

Occasionally he would ask the guide why he went a particular way. Albert would point out a broken twig or an overturned pebble the casual observer would miss.

Halfway up the next slope, Ray called to them. "Albert! Sheriff! Come look at this!"

Ray had wandered several yards from the trail Albert followed. Lansing tried not to be annoyed at this new distraction. When they reached Cabrera, he pointed at a mangled mess of fur and blood.

"What's that?" Lansing asked.

"My guess . . . it's what's left of that dog that went missing." Ray picked up a tuft of fur. "Looks like the stuff we found earlier."

Albert took a closer look. "I think you're right."

"That was nearly a mile away," Lansing observed. "How did the carcass end up here?"

"Some animal probably dragged it to this spot, then ate it." Albert said. "Other scavengers took their share. That's why there's only blood and fur."

"Any sign of a bear around here?" Lansing asked.

Both Cabreras looked around. "No, not really," Albert said. "Why?"

"Full grown German Shepherds weigh around seventy-five pounds. A bear is the only animal strong enough to carry that much weight. Even then they'd probably drag it."

"Well, bears and men," Ray commented. "We're tracking a man, right?"

"Why would someone carry a dead dog nearly a mile, just to throw it aside?"

The guides glanced at each other. The look on Ray Cabrera's face told Lansing the old tracker knew something. The sheriff started to make a comment when Albert cut him off.

"I think that's a mystery we can solve later. We need to keep moving while there's still daylight." He stepped past the sheriff, returning to the trail he was following.

Mystery, indeed, Lansing thought, following the younger guide.

"What happens if we catch up with this guy?" Ray asked. He didn't seem to struggle to keep up with the others.

"I need to find out why he attacked those boys. He chased them for at least a couple of miles in the middle of the night. He must have had a reason."

"Maybe he was just trying to scare them . . . kind of a prank."

"Could be."

"Are you going to arrest him?"

"I don't know yet. Those kids shot at him . . . We might be looking for a dead body."

"Yeah," Cabrera agreed. "A dead body."

Chapter Fifty-Eight

"Well, hello, Joy," Dorothy Gonzalez said when she answered the door. "What brings you out here?"

"Hi, Mrs. Gonzalez. The three of us wanted to speak to Eric."

"All three of you go to school with him?"

"No, ma'am. Only Serita and me." Joy gestured to Lincoln. "This is my brother. He's a wildlands firefighter."

"Goodness," the elder woman said, taking a closer look at the male in the group. "Were you hurt fighting the fire?"

"Yes, the first night." He saw no need to elaborate.

"Were you burned?"

"No, I broke my arm in a fall."

"That's terrible. I'm sorry.

"Anyway . . . Eric needs his rest," Dorothy Gonzalez said, returning to the original topic. "Can't you wait til Monday? He'll be at school."

"This really is important," Joy insisted. "It has to do with what happened yesterday."

"He needs to show us where the sheriff is," Lincoln added.

"Why?"

"He might be chasing the wrong people," the fireman offered. "Someone might get hurt."

"Please!" Joy pleaded.

The mother thought for a moment.

"I'll see if I can wake him . . . but if he doesn't want to get up, don't be surprised.

"Come in. You can wait in the living room."

Once inside, no one felt comfortable enough to sit.

Lincoln noticed a very young girl peeking around a corner. "Are you really a fireman?" she asked.

"I am," he nodded. "What's your name?"

"Edith . . ." She slid around the corner, her back against the wall. "But everybody calls me Edie."

Baca knelt on one knee. "Hello, Edie. My name is Lincoln, but my friends call me Linc."

"How did you hurt your arm?"

"I tripped and fell."

"Can I touch it?"

"Sure."

Edie ventured closer and placed her whole hand on the cast. "Does it hurt?"

"Not so much, anymore."

"I never saw a broken arm before."

"Edith!" her mother scolded as she entered from the hallway. "Leave that poor man alone."

"She's not bothering me," Lincoln said, standing.

"What did Eric say?" Joy asked anxiously.

"He's getting dressed. He'll be out in a minute." Dorothy placed her hand on her daughter's head to guide her. "Come on, Edie. Let's go in the kitchen."

Edie managed a quick wave to Lincoln before she disappeared through the door.

Almost immediately came the sound of bare feet slapping the floor of the hallway. Eric hurried into the room.

"Joy!" His excitement was noticeable.

"Eric!" She stepped closer and kissed him.

"Why are you here?"

"Can we go outside and talk?" Lincoln gestured toward the door.

"About what?"

"It's about what happened yesterday and last night." Joy held his hand and squeezed.

Chapter Fifty-Nine

Even though he wasn't completely convinced, Eric agreed to help Lincoln and the others intercept Sheriff Lansing. He knew it would be impossible to catch up by following the sheriff's current route. On a hunting map he showed how they could drive to Artiga, then follow dirt roads past Cerro Pelon. By that route, it was possible to reach Lansing and the two guides from the east.

Even though they didn't completely understand why Baca needed to find the sheriff, Eric assured his parents everything would be fine. He'd be with friends and promised they wouldn't take all night again.

There were misgivings when he approached the car with his rifle. He insisted it was for protection only. He wasn't hunting anything.

All four crowded into Serita's Citation . . . Joy and Eric in the backseat, Serita driving, Lincoln in the passenger seat because of the bulky cast.

***

Now that they were together, Eric and Lincoln could compare their experiences during the drive. Lincoln strained to look at the teen directly, finally giving up and facing forward while they talked.

Lincoln described his brief encounter with the four wild creatures on the mountain. The tallest one was over eight feet tall. The next tallest was seven feet in height. The last two were nearly that tall.

"In the Pueblo language they are called *atosle*. It's an ogre," Lincoln explained. "Supposedly they eat children, but my uncle said they're actually peaceful. The only reason they might attack a human is if we did harm to them first . . . them or one of their family."

The creatures he met didn't threaten him. The leader simply acknowledged his presence, then all four disappeared into the darkness.

Eric knitted his brows with concern. "Jerry's dog, Chulo, followed a scent from our farms. If they avoid humans, why did these *atosle* steal our animals?"

"The fire we started drove them from Cerro Grande. They might have had trouble finding food in an area new to them. Raiding your farms might not have been smart on their part, but for them it was better than starving.

"Joy said your friend shot one."

The look of concern never left Eric's face. "Adam shot . . . something."

"He thought it was a bear?"

"Yes . . . I did, too. I had it in my sights."

"What color was the fur?"

"I couldn't tell. It was in the shade."

"So, you shot a 'bear'. . ."

"We could tell it wasn't a bear after Adam shot it."

"How?"

"It screamed. It almost sounded human . . ."

"Then something started chasing you?"

"Not immediately." Eric described how they heard sticks striking tree trunks. Then there were whoops. When the *atosle* didn't get an answer, it came looking for its friend.

"We heard it crashing through the woods . . . and it was coming fast. We could hear saplings and branches being snapped. We took off before we could check on the thing we shot."

"So, it sounded like something big was coming?"

"Yeah. Definitely."

"When did your friends get hurt?"

"Jerry broke his ankle going down the first slope, but he's always been uncoordinated. Adam hurt his leg a couple of hours later."

"So, this *atosle* didn't attack your friends? I mean, he didn't physically hurt them, did he?"

"It threw fifty-pound rocks at us. One bounced and hit me," the senior protested.

"I realize that . . . but that happened after Jerry broke his ankle?"

"Yes."

"You three weren't moving very fast, then?"

"It took us all night to cover three or four miles."

"Did it attack you again?"

"No."

"Why not?"

"It knew we had guns. We shot at it. I might have hit it."

"But it still chased you, even after you shot at it?"

"Yes. All night."

"It could have attacked you again at any point," Lincoln observed. "You said you were moving slow. It could have come at you in the darkness and taken you all out . . . but it didn't."

"No . . . it didn't," Eric said slowly.

Lincoln had thought a lot about his conversation with Uncle Eluterio. He convinced himself these creatures only wanted to be left alone. Despite their size and appearance, *atosle* were not monsters.

"I don't think the *atosle* ever wanted to hurt any of you," Lincoln said. "I'll bet all it wanted to do was drive you away so you wouldn't bother its family anymore."

"But we're pretty sure it killed Chulo!"

"The dog probably didn't leave it much choice, did it?"

"No." Eric shook his head. "I guess not."

Once they reached Artiga, Gonzalez pointed out the county road they needed to take. Three miles south of Highway 15, their track climbed to higher ground and Cerro Pelon popped into view four miles away.

Chapter Sixty

Despite Albert Cabrera's prediction that his father would fall behind, Ray never did . . . plus, he constantly interrupted his son's tracking efforts.

"Come here, son! Look at this," became a phrase Lansing got tired of hearing. He didn't even bother looking himself after Ray beckoned a third time.

He had one more growing criticism of the old guide. Cabrera was becoming surlier. He started snapping at both Lansing and his son. He seemed to be reverting to the old Ray Cabrera. The only difference was he was sober. Lansing never saw him take a drink and he didn't reek of whiskey.

At the top of the next ridge, Ray insisted on another rest. Father and son knelt together for another family conference. Once again, Lansing found a tree some yards away to rest against. Checking his watch, it was five o'clock. They still had three hours of sunlight.

The Cabreras' conversation started off in low whispers. As it continued, the voices got louder, more argumentative. After almost fifteen minutes of back and forth, Albert finally stood. Lansing could clearly hear his words.

"I told you, I'll do anything to help mom!"

"Good," Ray growled, standing. "Then it's settled."

The sheriff had no idea what was settled. He didn't care. He was only interested in pressing on with their search.

Albert pulled out the map he'd displayed on the kitchen table.

"This next canyon is where the Gonzalez boy said someone threw those big rocks." He pointed to the mesa across the canyon. "Over there is as far as the teens went. That's where someone started chasing them."

Lansing nodded.

The sheriff and the younger Cabrera moved to the top of the slope. An animal trail delineated the edge. According to the contour lines, it was four hundred feet to the bottom of the canyon. On the descent the vegetation would be stunted. However, the gradient was shallow with the steepest portion being the first thirty or forty feet.

The sheriff was about to say something to the younger guide when he was struck from behind. The blow on the back of his head summersaulted him onto the slope.

Dazed, he tumbled for fifty feet, then slid another twenty, finally coming to rest against a juniper bush.

"Do you think he's dead?" Albert asked, peering at the lifeless body from above.

"We can only hope," Ray Cabrera said callously. "Let's go. It'll take a while to get to the next mesa and the day's not getting any younger."

Chapter Sixty-One

Halfway down the slope, Tito Calle realized he was not getting close to either suspect. They had split up and now were positioned to his left and right. He knew this because they started a new game . . . a sort of tag.

One would begin knocking a stick against a tree. Tito would head in that direction. The knocking would stop, and immediately start up again in the opposite direction.

After stumbling back and forth for a quarter of an hour, Calle had to rest. He sat with his head bowed, trying to catch his breath. He wished he had a bottle of water . . . no, a bottle of beer. The anger that drove him to pursue his tormentors had subsided.

Why bother? he thought. *You're never going to catch them. Go back, get in your truck, and go home, pendejo.*

He was hungry as well as thirsty. He admitted to himself he had been defeated. Not winning didn't bother him. He was used to losing. In fact, he considered that a kind of virtue. Sure, he got pushed around. But life wasn't a struggle if you let other people make your decisions for you . . . Luis at work, Linda at home, Jimmy the rest of the time.

Well, Jimmy not so much now, he thought. *No* . . . he corrected himself. *Jimmy not at all! Not anymore.*

Tito was suddenly overcome with a sense of loss. Jimmy was gone. His best friend . . . his brother-in-law . . . was dead. He forgot all about how he mistreated Ramona. He forgot how Jimmy constantly picked on him . . . treated him like crap.

Tito's eyes stung. Jimmy was dead and he killed him. He didn't get much time to wallow in his guilt, though.

His thoughts were interrupted when a stone struck him in the middle of his back. It stung so much he thought he had been shot.

Tito jumped up and turned around. The rock had come from further up the slope. He started to yell at the attacker when a rock from the right struck his cheek. His hand automatically covered the spot where he was hit as he turned toward the second attacker.

A whoop came from above him. He looked up. Another rock pelted him on his left shoulder.

Calle realized he was no longer the hunter. He was now the prey. To get to his truck, he had to go back up the slope. He knew that wasn't an option as his assailants whooped to each other and continued hurling rocks. (Why they whooped and didn't simply yell was a mystery he didn't have time to ponder.)

Turning to run down the slope, Tito tripped, sprawling face down. The stones kept coming. He struggled to his feet and began making his way through the dense woods. Because of the slope and the trees, he couldn't run. He hurried as fast as he dared, though. The whoops continued behind him, getting closer.

If rocks were thrown, he didn't notice. He descended another two hundred feet before reaching the treeless canyon floor.

He hesitated, unsure which direction to take. He realized he couldn't run on the rock strewn, dry creek bed. Not very fast anyway. But he was in the open now. Why should he have to run? His assailants would have to leave the protection of the forest.

He pulled the Buck knife from his belt and opened the blade. He could confront his tormentors now. Convinced he would only face a couple of teenagers he would stand his ground.

Tito faced the forest. No more rocks were flying at him. He couldn't hear any sound from his pursuers. There was a chance they had given up. Maybe they saw his knife. Maybe they were actually afraid of him.

"Okay, *muchachos,* you want to play?" he shouted. "I'm ready. Come on. Show yourselves. You're so brave when you can hide behind trees. I'll take you both on. *Mano a mano.*"

Calle stared at the trees for several minutes. There was no response, no movement, no sound.

Positive he had won, Tito folded the blade and returned it to its belt case. About to start back up the slope, he heard a grunt come from his left.

He looked and saw, fifty feet away, a . . .? He had no words to describe it.

Another grunt came from behind him.

He wheeled around. An identical looking creature stood just twenty feet away.

Tito screamed, "Get away from me!"

Calle started running back to the protection of the forest. He didn't know if he was being chased. He scrambled up the slope as fast as he could. He didn't stop or slow down. All he wanted was distance between himself and the things he saw on the canyon floor.

Nearly to the top of the ridge, he looked up to see how far he had to go.

Standing at the rim, bathed in shadows, were the two creatures he thought he left behind.

Tito screamed, "NO!"

He fell backwards as his attackers pounced for a final assault.

Chapter Sixty-Two

Albert Cabrera convinced himself he was helping Ray for the sake of his mother. There was more to it, though. For twenty years he bent to his father's demands. He never knew if the senior Cabrera was kind deep inside. There must have been something that attracted Bess to the beast.

It's said the eyes are the window of the soul. Albert wasn't sure his father even had a soul. All he ever remembered seeing was whiskey-soaked anger with a streak of mean as wide as the Rio Grande was long.

When he ran into Ray that morning, Albert couldn't believe how pleasant the encounter had been. From the time he picked him up at the ranch through the hike up Little Creek Canyon, his father seemed normal. He didn't joke or kid around . . . Albert didn't think the old man was capable of that much normality. But he wasn't surly . . . not at first.

Ray began to change after he found the first footprint. It looked human but it was huge. Easily fifteen inches long and eight inches across. At their first rest stop, Albert tried to convince the old tracker there was nothing to the track. His father argued differently.

"I'll show you," Ray hissed. "There will be lots more."

Albert studied his father's face as they talked. There was something different . . . in the eyes. There was that ever-present cruelty bubbling up from inside. But there was also a wildness he'd never seen before.

When Ray kept calling him back to see what he'd discovered, Albert placated him, though he wasn't sure why. He was also surprised that the senior guide was correct. There were more tracks. They weren't as well defined as the first one Ray saw. But it was obvious they were following something big.

"You know exactly what it is," Ray whispered. They knelt together, supposedly for a second rest.

Albert shook his head. "They've supposedly been spotted around the San Juan River. But nothing this far south."

He watched his father's eyes. The wildness had morphed into craziness. The more they talked, the crazier Ray became. His stare was intense. Albert could feel it boring into him.

"If we track this son-of-a bitch down and kill it . . ." Ray said. "Don't you realize what that would be worth?"

"I don't know, Dad . . ."

Both men were surprised Albert used the term. Albert took it as a sign he was reverting back to his youth when Ray could intimidate him.

Ray considered it as proof he was winning the discussion.

"The sheriff isn't going let us kill a creature like that!"

"How's he going to stop us? There's only one of him."

The argument went back and forth for ten minutes. The rhetoric became harsher, louder.

Albert was taken completely off-guard when Ray offered a solution.

"Who says we even need Lansing? These canyons are pretty steep. People have accidents all the time."

"You're saying we should kill him?"

"Not shoot him . . . just help him over the edge. It probably won't kill him."

"I'm not getting involved with murder!"

"Listen . . ." Ray growled, grabbing his son's wrist. "I'm desperate. You don't know this, but your mother and I are about to lose the ranch . . ."

Albert pulled free. "I know all about the ranch . . ."

"How do you know?"

"Mom told me!"

Cabrera stared at his son, his face getting redder and redder. He looked like a man about to have a stroke.

"I will do anything to save my place . . ." he said through clenched teeth. "What we're tracking is nothing more than a wild animal. You can help me or not . . . I don't care. I'm going to find this thing . . . shoot it . . . and cut off its head.

"I'll sell it for a million bucks . . . Hell, I'll sell it to the highest bidder . . . I'll get ten million bucks."

Ray stopped and let his words sink in. Albert didn't look convinced.

Cabrera's next words came out low and guttural. "If you can't come around to my way of thinking . . ." He paused for effect. "I can't make any promises about your mom's future . . . I mean with us losing the ranch and all . . ."

Albert couldn't tell if that was a genuine threat against his mother or not. Ray looked crazy enough to do anything . . . He was ready to kill the sheriff. What would another body mean to him?

The young guide quickly reviewed his options. He could beat the crap out of the old man for threatening his mother, but that wouldn't remove Ray as a threat. He could shoot him . . . which didn't seem wise in front of Lansing. Or he could go along with his father's scheme.

He brushed away the thought of telling the sheriff about Ray's plan. He was suddenly overcome with greed. The old man said they could make ten million dollars. His share would be five million . . . plus the prestige of tracking down the most elusive creature on the planet.

At twenty-five he could be the most famous hunting guide in New Mexico . . . maybe the entire country.

He stood. He made his statement sound like he only had altruistic motives. "I told you, I'll do anything to help mom!"

"Good," Ray growled, standing. "Then it's settled."

186

***

Even with both expert trackers plying their trade, the trail was difficult to follow. There was an urgency in their search, now. There was less than three hours of daylight left. If they didn't find their quarry before dark, it might disappear forever.

Little time was spent on the downward slope. They knew the creature was heading for the bottom of the canyon. It would be more important to find where it climbed up the opposite slope.

Neither checked the sheriff's condition. He might or might not be dead. There was plenty of time to concoct a believable story on how the accident happened. They had more important things on their agenda.

Ray was correct in estimating it would take an hour to reach the top of the opposite mesa. At the edge of a meadow, they found where the boys rested. There was trash from a meal, plenty of trampled grass, even a spent rifle shell.

There were also large footprints. They came from and led back to the tree line on the opposite side of the clearing.

Neither man said a thing. As guides, they knew any conversation could alert their prey, whether it was elk or pheasant.

They entered the next stretch of forest. A few yards in, they found disturbed pine needles and several broken branches. At the same time, they both spotted a small, red stain on the ground. Experience told them it was blood.

They looked at each other and nodded. This explained the rifle shell.

The Gonzalez boy had been less than truthful about what had happened. They had shot something.

Was it the same creature that chased them all night? Was it a different one? If that was the case, how many could be wandering the forest?

The Cerro Grande Fire had displaced hundreds, maybe thousands of animals. These creatures were part of the mix, driven from their lairs.

Leading away from the blood, there was a swath of broken branches and saplings . . . a highway for the hunting guides to follow. They hurried their pace. Their quarry might be close.

Chapter Sixty-Three

After they passed Cerro Pelon, the dirt road split. Right took them north. Left took them south.

"What now?" Serita asked.

Eric strained to look out. "The mountain was north of us. We should turn left."

Serita did as instructed. Eric watched behind them, trying to estimate how far they needed to go south. Two hundred yards down the new road, the driver stopped.

"Yeah. This is good," Eric said. "How'd you guess?"

"I stopped because there's a tire rim in the road."

"That's all right. We can get out here," Eric suggested.

"I'm not leaving my car in the middle of this road."

"I'll get out and move the rim," Lincoln said. "There's a side road over there. You can park on it."

Lincoln, Joy, and Eric all piled out. Baca had no problem picking up the ten-pound wheel and tossing it aside.

"That looks brand new," Eric said. "I bet it hasn't been here long."

"You sure I should leave my car here?" Silva asked after she parked. "There's a truck up there." She gestured toward the hill.

Lincoln walked over to inspect. "They have plenty of room to drive around. I think you'll be okey."

"All right, if you say so." She grabbed her handbag and locked her car.

"You sure you want to carry that?" Lincoln asked.

"I want my I.D. with me just in case they need to identify my body."

"What do you think is going to happen?"

"I don't know . . . How tall is that thing you saw?"

"Eight feet."

"What if we run into it before we find the sheriff?"

"Don't worry," Lincoln reassured her. "We won't run into it. The *atosle* will hear us before we even get close."

They joined Joy and Eric. Lincoln gestured toward the forest.

"Lead the way."

Eric eyed the firefighter's cast. "You sure you're up for this?"

"I can take care of myself!"

"And I'm here to help him," Serita added.

***

At the far edge of the woods, Eric pointed out another chrome rim. No one could guess why it was there.

Lincoln's bravado was tested on the first slope. Serita wanted to position herself behind him in case he slipped or fell. Baca knew if he did fall, she could never stop him.

"Serita, it would be better for both of us if you didn't do that. Just stay close in case I need a helping hand."

His prediction was correct. His center of gravity had shifted because of the cast strapped across his body. It wasn't until halfway up the ridge that his body adjusted to its new reality. Until then, Serita grabbed his free hand three times to keep him from falling backwards.

Once Lincoln was sure on his feet, he growled at the poor girl for pawing at him.

"I'm just trying to help," she whined.

"I don't need your help," he snapped. "I can do this by myself!"

Silva wanted to point out he would be at the bottom of the hill if she hadn't assisted him. Instead, she bit her lip. She was finally with the man she'd had a crush on for a year. She could put up with a little abuse . . . for a while, anyway.

The treeless ridge top provided a view of the surrounding landscape. Cerro Pelon, three miles away, towered a thousand feet above their position. Directly west was another ridge/mesa. Eric pulled out his hunting map for reference.

"That next ridge is as far as we got," he said, pointing the way. "If the sheriff isn't there yet, we can wait."

"How long will it take to get there?" Joy asked.

"Maybe an hour."

Eric led the way again. It would be four hundred feet down, and another four hundred feet up to the top of the next ridge. Straight down the slope would be too steep for Baca, so Eric chose a zigzag route.

At the halfway point he brought the tiny column to a halt.

"What's wrong?" Joy asked.

"There's something ahead. You and the others wait here for a minute . . . let me check it out."

As he stepped forward, he unslung his rifle from his shoulder. In the deepening shadows, he thought he saw clothing on their intended path. It could be nothing more than lost shirt or jacket, but he wanted to be cautious.

As he drew nearer, Eric froze in his tracks. He saw it was indeed clothing . . . bloody clothing . . . and the owner still wore them.

Chapter Sixty-Four

With less than thirty miles from the center of Santa Fe to the Cerro Grande Fire, the column of smoke was an ever-present smudge on the northern horizon. For Tina Morales, having to cope with the traffic and the haze on the highway when they approached the wildfire was merely an inconvenience. She and Marta couldn't imagine how miserable it must be living downwind.

Though it was past 5:00, neither was particularly hungry once they finished shopping. If they needed, they could grab a bite when they drove through Segovia.

The traffic in Santa Fe hadn't lessened any, even as they intercepted Highway 15/285.

The cars and trucks finally started thinning out once they passed the turnoff to Tesuque Village. The speed limit increased to sixty-five, which also helped.

Two boys, five or six, faced backwards and waved at the teachers from an older, red Ford Escort. Marta waved back. Tina watched the rearview mirror, looking for an opportunity to slide into the passing lane.

Both were startled by a loud bang. A flash of dust exploded from the front right tire of the Escort. The driver stomped on her brakes and struggled for control. The car swerved to the right, grinding metal on metal along the guardrail.

Tina mashed her brakes as well. A semi to her left prevented her from escaping in that direction. She pointed her truck toward the shoulder, hoping to avoid an accident. The sound of squealing tires and brakes sounded behind her. The teachers braced for the impact that followed a second later. More crashes continued as the pile-up continued.

The F-150 stopped only a foot from the red Escort. Seven more cars and pickups had joined the derby, with varying degrees of damage. Tina's first concern was for the two boys who waved at her. She jumped from the cab and ran to the crumpled car against the rail.

An airbag had deployed for the driver . . . the only one in the car. She struggled to push it out of the way, her face powdered with dust.

Tina yanked the door open. Three boys were crying in the back seat. Both the driver and the front passenger appeared dazed. *Thank God,* Tina thought. *At least they're alive.*

"Are you all right?"

The driver shook her head. "I—I don't know." She immediately attempted to turn toward the kids in the backseat. The airbag and seat-belt constrained her. "Jimmy!" she screamed. "My baby! Are you all right?"

"Mommy!" The pitiful response was mixed with sobbing.

The other two boys joined the chorus, "Mommy!"

"Here," Tina said anxiously. "Let me help you out."

With the airbag now deflated, Tina could reach across and unbuckle the seatbelt. As she supported the driver as she got out, the female passenger started yelling:

"I can't get out! I can't get out!"

The Escort's right side was crushed against the metal railing.

"Just a minute," Tina barked. "You'll have to come out this way."

Once she was out of her seat, the driver immediately tried to crowd Tina out of the way.

"I have to get my baby!"

Even though they were the same height, the driver outweighed her rescuer by thirty pounds. Tina struggled against her.

"Please," Tina pleaded. "I'm trying to help."

Marta suddenly appeared. Knowing she was no match for the frantic mother, she grabbed the woman's hair from behind and yanked. The driver nearly fell backwards. This gave Tina enough space to reach inside and unbuckle the passenger's seatbelt.

"Can you move?"

The passenger nodded. "I think I can."

"Then climb out this way," Morales ordered. "Then we'll get the boys."

Sirens could be heard in the distance. Help was on the way.

Chapter Sixty-Five

As consciousness crept into his brain, Cliff Lansing began to realize he hurt . . . he hurt all over. He associated his headache with a sharp pain at the back of his neck.

He squeezed his eyes open, trying to remember where he was. He found himself lying face up, staring into juniper branches.

He couldn't sit up. The bush was in his way. He strained to roll over but quickly realized he was on a hill of some type. Using his elbows and pushing with his heels, he wriggled from beneath the branch canopy.

The deep blue of the New Mexico sky greeted him. Managing to sit up, he got his bearings. He was on the slope of a canyon. Turning to look up toward the top was painful. The rim was fifty, maybe sixty feet above him.

It was early evening. The canyon was already enveloped in deep shadow. A waft of cool air brushed his face, and he was glad he wore his jacket.

Jacket! Why am I wearing my jacket?

He inspected himself. He was in his uniform. A pant leg was torn. A smear of blood oozed from a scrape on his knee.

I must have fallen. That explained why he hurt. *I must have fallen down this slope. How could I have done that?*

He tried to stand. Dizziness stopped him.

While the unsteadiness passed, he would try to remember how he ended up in a canyon. It didn't take long. He was tracking a person or persons responsible for attacking three teens. Two hunting guides were helping him . . . the Cabreras . . . father and son.

They had stopped for a rest. Albert . . . Albert showed him a map. He pointed to the opposite side of the canyon. That's where they were going.

Lansing tried to remember what happened next. It was a blank.

He went from standing at the edge of the canyon to being under a juniper tree fifty feet down. He was pushed! That could be the only explanation.

Why didn't he remember falling?

He gingerly touched the back of his head. A bump. The source of the pain he woke up to. No . . . he wasn't pushed. A whack against his skull sent him down the slope.

He was talking to Albert. Ray must have hit him!

"That worthless piece of crap," he mumbled. "Why, Ray? What the hell is going on?"

He managed to stand, prodded by a growing anger. He looked around. His Stetson was nowhere to be seen. His rifle lay on the slope twenty feet above him.

He checked his watch . . . 5:50. He had been knocked out cold for most of an hour.

Stumbling up the slope, he retrieved his weapon. His pistol was still in its holster. His head gradually cleared.

He marveled at the fact that he wasn't injured any more than he was after the fall. The heavy jacket helped cushion him. He had scraped his knee, but nothing serious. He was more upset at losing a pair of uniform trousers.

There was no point in climbing back to the top of the mesa. His attacker was gone. The guides were on their way to the opposite side of the canyon.

Lansing started down the slope. A hundred feet down he found his hat resting against the low hanging branches of a scrub spruce.

It was an unfortunate truth, but he admitted he felt partially un-dressed if he wasn't wearing his cattleman's hat. He still had a full head of hair, so he wasn't hiding baldness. Wearing his hat was his identity . . . it was who he was. If that was vanity on his part, he really didn't care. He could live with it . . . as long as he had his hat.

The hat also boosted his confidence. He seriously considered a tac-tical retreat until he had reinforcements. He guessed he had been left for dead, though . . . which meant he had the element of surprise. The last thing the trackers would expect would be him showing up now to arrest them.

As he worked his way to the canyon floor, he kept asking himself *Why did they attack me?*

Chapter Sixty-Six

"Did you check for a pulse?" Lincoln Baca asked after Eric reported his discovery.

"Why? He looked dead to me," Gonzalez protested.

"Let's go see," the firefighter insisted.

Eric led the way to the bloody corpse. Joy and Serita remained where they were, neither one interested in seeing a dead body.

"Help me turn him over," Baca ordered.

Once he was face up, there was no doubt the man was dead. The body had been ripped open . . . the face mauled. A few flies were interrupted from gorging on the congealed blood.

"See if he has a wallet." Lincoln had taken charge of the situation.

Kneeling, Eric first produced a set of keys from the front. Feeling underneath, he found the wallet in the back pocket. He stood and opened it.

"His name is Calle . . . Tito Calle. He lives in Segovia."

"*Lived* in Segovia," Baca corrected. "We need to give those things to the sheriff. I wonder if that was his truck back there."

"What truck?"

"It was up the hill from where Serita parked."

Eric shoved the wallet and keys into his jacket. "What did this?"

"Probably a bear . . ."

"You sure it's not one of those *atosle*?"

Lincoln could not be sure of anything. "Why would you say that?"

"Because there's no sign of a bear around here."

"There's no sign of an *atosle*, either." He stepped closer to Eric. "Listen, until we know better, just tell the girls it was a bear attack . . . that you have a rifle, and they have nothing to worry about."

"That won't stop me from worrying. If it was an *atosle*, is this rifle enough to defend us?"

"You thought you shot one last night. It didn't attack you after that."

"No, I guess not."

"What are you two doing over there?" Joy shouted.

"We're coming!" Lincoln yelled. Then to Eric, "A bear . . . right?"

"Yeah, okay."

"Let's turn him back over," Lincoln said.

***

"We should go home," Serita whimpered. "It's not safe out here."

"We're almost there," Lincoln reassured her, giving her a tight squeeze with his good arm.

"It's going to be dark pretty soon," she protested. "I hate bears . . . and what if we run into one of your *atosle* things? I'm scared!"

Joy was having her own doubts about their expedition.

"Why don't Serita and I go back to the car and wait for you . . . while we still have daylight?"

"We need to stick together," Lincoln said firmly. "You could get lost."

He almost said, "Something might attack you," but quickly realized those would be a poor choice of words. "At least Eric has a gun for protection. Right, Eric?"

"Linc's right. We need to stick together."

The girls nodded, reluctantly.

"If we hurry," Eric pressed, "we can get to the top of the next ridge in forty-five minutes."

Eric continued his zigzag route to the canyon floor, avoiding the dead body. It was less than an hour until sunset. The shadows seemed darker as they descended further.

At the bottom, no one was interested in resting. All four wanted to get through the ordeal as quickly as possible.

"I don't know why you just didn't tell the sheriff you were chased by these *atosle*," Serita whined as they started up the next slope. "Then we wouldn't have to be out here."

"Well, I never saw what was chasing us, did I, Serita?" Eric snapped. "And I didn't know about the *atosle* till Linc told me about them."

"But you knew it wasn't some man . . . Why didn't you say that when you were asked?"

Eric half-agreed with his classmate about not wanting to be out there. He was tired. More tired than he ever remembered being. Joy Baca was the only reason he was in the woods that afternoon . . . any excuse to be with her. If he had been honest with the sheriff, he'd be home in bed. But then he wouldn't be with Joy.

"What's done is done," Lincoln growled, intervening.

He was putting too much strain on his broken collar bone. Climbing up and down steep inclines was NOT what the doctor ordered. Baca was hurting, and he had a growing fear he would do permanent damage.

Despite the pain he pushed himself. The Cerro Grande Fire was caused by careless men. It was caused by his firefighting crew . . . by him. He personally felt responsible for what happened to the human-like creatures he saw that first night. He needed to make sure Sheriff Lansing and the two hunting guides didn't harm any *atosle*.

Chapter Sixty-Seven

Lansing stared up at the wooded slope from the canyon floor. The forest looked thicker, more forbidding than the other trees he had climbed through that day. He reassured himself the issue was perception. It was late in the day. Shade had morphed into deep shadows. He didn't know when late afternoon slipped into early evening. He guessed sunset marked the transition.

Standing four hundred feet below the ridge tops, he couldn't tell if sunlight still lit the tips of the highest peaks. According to his watch, official sunset was an hour away. Even so, once he reached the top, there wouldn't be much time to track Ray Cabrera and his son.

What the hell do you think you're doing? he asked himself as he started into the trees. *You're acting like a damned rookie!*

His initial impulse to go after the Cabreras was driven by anger. That pique had subsided somewhat once he reached the canyon floor. Rational thinking began to creep in.

What if he did catch up with them? What then? Did he plan on marching them up and down these steep canyons at gunpoint? How could he be sure they couldn't get the upper hand and finish him off?

Was he only being driven by pride?

Had Cabrera knocked out all of his common sense?

The debate inside him raged back and forth as he climbed higher. He could feel his confidence waning as well. That was a feeling foreign to him. He had always trusted his instincts.

The closer he got to the top of the ridge, the more his resolve waivered.

Then came the unmistakable "pop" of a distant rifle shot. Seconds later several "pops" sounded in quick succession. As nearly as Lansing could tell, they came from above.

Whatever doubt he had in his logic immediately disappeared.

Something was going on. Someone was probably in trouble. His instincts told him he was right to continue his climb.

A new set of questions surfaced. If the shots were fired by the Cabreras, who were they shooting at?

On the other hand, someone might be shooting at the father and son team. Was it the same people who chased the teens the night before?

Whichever the case, he would be walking into gunfire. He already knew Ray and Albert Cabrera were a problem. Now, there might be more threats to watch for.

When Lansing finally reached the top of the canyon, the forest thinned out. The trees were still numerous enough to provide cover if needed, plus they would mask his approach.

The sun was sinking fast, and twilight wouldn't last long.

Chapter Sixty-Eight

The canyon floor sported a creek that ran intermittently and thick vegetation. The slope where they found Tito Calle saw ample rainfall as well. The pines and spruce were so thick no one could see more than thirty feet ahead . . . sometimes less.

The new slope was almost barren in comparison. The hearty plants, mostly varieties of juniper, seldom grew much more than six feet in height. Dry grasses tried to fill the ten-to-twenty-foot gaps between the trees masquerading as bushes.

If he had been alone, Gonzalez would have chosen a more direct route to the next ridge top. For the sake of his companions, he stuck to the zigzag strategy. It was easier on the girls, and Linc Baca looked like he was suffering, though he said nothing.

"What happens when we reach the top?" Joy asked her brother.

"We look around and see if the sheriff is there."

"Eric," Lincoln called to their guide, "are there a lot of trees up there?"

"In spots. There are open areas too."

"What if your sheriff isn't there, Linc?" Serita whined. "How long are we supposed to wait for him to show up?"

"I don't know!" Baca shouted. His collar hurt and he regretted bringing Silva on their hike. After her constant complaining, he decided there was no chance the two would ever date.

Serita recoiled at the harsh response. Her image of the valiant fire-fighter evaporated. If that's the way he treats her on their first "date," she wasn't sure she wanted a second. He was mean. If he shouted at her in the company of others, how would he treat her when they were alone.

Lincoln saw the expression on her face. He instantly regretted speaking to her that way. He thought of himself as a nice person. He never yelled at anyone.

"Serita, I'm sorry . . . I didn't mean to yell at you." He wanted to blame his pain for his words. Instead, he said, "I'm worried we won't find the sheriff . . . I'm afraid we'll be too late and one of the *atosle* might be killed. If that happens . . . it will be my fault."

Serita melted at the look on Baca's face. There was real pain . . . deep pain. Not just physical hurt, either. His eyes betrayed genuine kindness. She stepped closer and touched his right arm as she kissed him.

The quartet had stopped in their tracks when Lincoln shouted. Eric and Joy watched the scene play out. Though glad there was a happy ending, they didn't want things to turn too romantic . . . not now.

"This really isn't a good make out place," Eric observed.

"After we're finished, you two can get a room," Joy said. "Right now, we still have some hiking to do."

Embarrassed, Serita took a step back.

Lincoln barely heard the remarks. The kiss was unexpected . . . and surprisingly . . . he tried to find the right word . . . wonderful.

"Come on," Eric insisted. "We're halfway up."

"Right," Baca said, regaining his composure. "Let's go."

The group had taken no more than a dozen steps when they heard the "pop" of a single gunshot. A moment later they heard several more shots.

They looked from one to another. Joy said what the others were thinking.

"We're too late!"

"Maybe not," her brother said, hopefully. "We need to get up there and find out what's going on."

Eric led the way. Their steps crunched on loose stones and dried grass. Just a few minutes after the last gunshot, Gonzalez held up his hand.

"Sh-h . . . Did you hear that?"

The others strain to hear anything.

"What?" Joy asked.

"I thought I heard a scream."

Chapter Sixty-Nine

Tina couldn't help but feel sorry for Ramona Clay, the driver who had the blowout. Her car looked like it was a total loss. Her son, Jimmy Jr., was at the bottom of a three-boy pileup in the back seat of the Escort. Once he was extracted from the car, he complained of neck pain.

When the ambulance arrived, the EMTs secured the five-year-old on a hard board for transport. He needed to be examined in an emergency room to determine the extent of his injury. The nearest hospital was Christus St. Vincent in Santa Fe.

Ramona tried to maintain a brave face for her son, but she couldn't keep the silent tears from flowing. Her companion put her arms around her for comfort.

Tina unashamedly listened in on the conversation.

"Linda, I don't know what's going to happen," Ramona whimpered. "I don't know how bad Jimmy's hurt. I don't have any money if he has to stay in the hospital. And if they say he can go home, how am I supposed to get back to Segovia?"

"Don't worry, *mija*. Tito's probably home by now. I'll see if I can find a phone and call him. He would be glad to help you . . . you know that."

Ramona nodded. "I know." She paused and took a deep breath. "Jimmy's going to kill me, isn't he?"

"Your husband is not going to kill anyone . . . Tito and I will make sure of that."

"Ma'am," one of the emergency technicians interrupted, "we're ready to go. You can ride in the back with your son."

The two women said their goodbyes and Ramona rode off in the ambulance.

"Excuse me," Tina said stepping forward. "My name's Tina Morales. I heard you talking with your friend. Are those your boys over there?" She gestured toward Linda Calle's sons.

Linda nodded. "Yes. Why?"

"If you need a ride to Segovia, I'm heading that way."

"Actually," Calle hesitated. "I'm Linda Calle. If you have a cell phone, could I borrow it? I'll call my husband and he can pick us up."

"Sure." She opened her handbag and dug through it. A moment later she handed her phone to Linda.

The woman stared at the device, trying to decipher its operation.

"Here, let me dial the number for you."

Linda gladly returned the phone. When Tina was ready, she recited her home number. As soon as the phone at the other end began ringing, Tina gave the phone back.

Calle listened through six rings. Her face clouded with concern as she closed the clamshell. "I don't know where he is. He should be home by now."

"Well, my offer still stands," Tina said. She nodded toward her truck. "We have plenty of room."

"I guess that'll be all right," Linda agreed. "My husband should be home by then."

***

Despite being struck from behind, there was no visible damage to the F-150. The car that plowed into the truck's bumper wasn't as fortunate. After hitting Tina's truck in the front and getting slammed from behind, the Honda Civic was no longer drivable. In fact, four of the eight cars in the pileup needed towing.

Highway Patrol cars and ambulances clogged the stretch of road. Traffic was diverted through Tesuque Village. A dozen tow trucks parked along the shoulder waiting patiently, hoping for a chance at a customer. Drivers stood next to their cars, trading insurance information. A few talked on cell phones, explaining why they were late or looking for rides.

The driver of the Honda Civic appeared to think he was going to make some easy money when he discovered Morales didn't own the truck. His greed was short lived when she showed him the insurance papers. Clifford Lansing, Tina Morales, and an Oscar Vega were all listed as insured operators of the truck.

Tina didn't mention that the owner was the sheriff of San Phillipe County. She saved that bit of information, just in case she needed it. It turned out, she didn't.

Ultimately, no citations were issued.

It took two hours for the metal mess to be untangled. Linda directed the tow truck driver to take Ramona's car to *Luis' Car Repair and Body Shop* in Segovia. He was miffed that he wouldn't see immediate payment. A Highway Patrol officer threatened him with a ticket if he didn't remove the disabled car as requested.

Tina introduced Marta, and Linda presented her sons. After shopping bags were rearranged, Linda, Juan, and Roberto Calle climbed into the back seat of the crew cab. The sun was setting, and it would soon be dark. The red-orange glow of the Cerro Grande Fire dominated the horizon as they drove north.

Chapter Seventy

"Do you think your friend's son is going to be all right?" Marta asked once they were heading down the road.

"He's my nephew," Linda said. "Ramona's my sister-in-law . . . but, yes, I think he'll be just fine."

"So, you've known Ramona a long time, then." Tina had joined the conversation.

"We were in school together. My husband and I have been sweet-hearts since tenth grade."

"Oh, that's nice," Marta said, smiling.

"I heard her mention a Jimmy." Tina glanced in the rearview mirror to see Linda's face.

"Yeah," Linda nodded as she looked out the side window. "That's her husband."

"Does she really think he'll hurt her?"

Linda took a deep breath. "She's his favorite piñata . . . but he took off drinking Tuesday night and hasn't come home yet. I'm hoping he never comes home . . . I think she does too."

"Did she report him missing?"

"No, not yet. But she checked the hospitals to make sure he wasn't hurt. She even called the police to see if he was arrested. No one's seen him."

"What about his friends or coworkers?"

"The only friend he has is my husband plus they work together. Tito said he hasn't seen him since Tuesday evening when they had a beer together. I'm hoping he drank himself to death."

"I take it you don't like him."

"Jimmy Clay is a pig. He's even worse when he's drunk. Of course, he's not drunk when he's at work or asleep, so, he's not drunk all the time." Her words intertwined bitterness and sarcasm.

"Why doesn't Ramona leave him?"

"He has her convinced she's fat and ugly. No other man will have her . . . Besides, he won't let her take his son away."

The truck cab filled with an uncomfortable silence.

"We teach," Marta finally said. "Up in Las Palmas. We're high school teachers."

Linda nodded. "That's good. What do you teach?"

"I teach English. Tina teaches chemistry."

"O-oh." Roberto became interested when the conversation went in a new direction. "Is chemistry hard?"

"It's not so bad if you study," Tina admitted. "Are you in school?"

"I'm going into second grade next year."

"Wow! Do you like school?"

"Oh, yes," the six-year-old lied. "I do."

"What do you like most?"

"Soccer."

Both teachers smiled. Tina realized her question should have been more specific. She should have asked what subjects he liked. Of course, grade school might have changed. They might be teaching soccer as a subject now, though she had her doubts.

Juan suddenly felt left out. "I'm in kindergarten."

"That's great," Marta said.

The school topic was quickly exhausted, and the boys fell silent.

"What does your husband do?" Tina asked.

"He's a mechanic . . . but he can do almost anything. He's good with his hands."

"He wasn't at work this late, was he?"

210

"He's always picking up extra jobs. We're trying to save up to buy a house. Our trailer is getting crowded."

"With two growing boys, I'll bet it is."

The traffic had thinned out after passing the turnoff to Las Alamos. As they approached Segovia, Calle directed Tina off the highway toward the center of town. It wasn't long before they reached Milagro Village Mobile Home Park.

It had been dark for some time, and Linda was shocked her husband wasn't home yet. As she and the boys climbed out of the truck, Tina wrote something on a scrap of paper. She handed it to Linda.

"This is my name and number," she said. "If you or Ramona need help with anything, please call me."

"Thanks." Calle took the paper, then ushered her boys toward the dark trailer. She wasn't sure what kind of help a chemistry teacher could offer.

Tina hadn't mentioned she lived with the county sheriff. She didn't advertise that information for a lot of reasons . . . her protection . . . Lansing's protection. It was also a way to avoid people making unreasonable requests.

As they navigated their way back to Highway 15, the Cerro Grande Fire lit up the skies to the west, visible even through the haze of smoke that blanketed Segovia.

Chapter Seventy-One

Lansing knew Valles Caldera was the heart of the Jemez Mountains. North of the giant crater all streams, permanent or otherwise, flowed into the Cohino River. The Cohino joined the Rio Grande on the San Juan Pueblo Reservation two miles north of Segovia, the waters eventually reaching the Gulf of Mexico.

The mesas and ridge lines tapered to nothing as their canyons converged. The mesas seldom reached a mile across. The ridges, sometimes called mesitas, were never more than a few hundred feet wide.

The sheriff realized he was not on a mesa. Recalling Albert Cabrera's map, this ridge continued north for no more than two thousand feet. How far south it extended he had no idea. Anything happening on that mesita, though, must have happened to the south, in the direction of the gunfire. That's the direction he started his search.

Shafts of light from the setting sun shot between the trees. Lansing tried to find any hint of a trail. Widening his search back and forth, the lengthening shadows didn't help.

On the far side of the mesita, as the last of the light sank below the distant mountains, he found a swath of broken saplings and branches. He knew the two guides hadn't caused the destruction. Whatever did cause it provided a trail for the Cabreras to follow.

It also gave Lansing a trail to follow, even in the fading light. He mentally kicked himself in the butt for not bringing his own flashlight. Both of the guides carried one. He figured if their search extended into the night, he would be covered.

As twilight engulfed the mountains, an eerie red-orange glow lit the sky to the southeast. The Cerro Grande Fire had now raged for eleven days. It had moved onto the Santa Clara Pueblo Reservation and now

San Phillipe County. He wondered how much more destruction the wildfire would cause before it was stamped out.

One problem at a time, the sheriff admonished himself. He couldn't let his mind wander. He was tracking two men who tried to kill him. He couldn't afford to be distracted, even with his own thoughts.

As twilight faded to darkness, the trail became harder to follow. His efforts to move quietly became more difficult. His progress was slow.

Just as he contemplated stopping until daylight, another distraction erupted. Somewhere behind him someone was shouting.

"Sheriff Lansing! Can you hear me? Sheriff Lansing!"

Chapter Seventy-Two

It was dark by the time the foursome reached the top of the little mesa. The quarter moon provided no useful light. The stars sparkled against a cloudless sky. To the southeast, the wildfire illuminated the smoke clouds like a small city lit by red lanterns.

Eric stared at the horizon. Joy joined him, taking his hand in hers.

"This is the first time I've seen the fire at night," he admitted. "It looks bad."

"It is." She squeezed his hand. "It's reached Pueblo lands. My mom wouldn't let us take the truck just in case the fire got too close . . . in case they have to leave in a hurry." She looked at him. "You didn't see the fire last night?"

"Last night we were worried about other things."

Lincoln and Serita joined them. "Where should we start looking for the sheriff?"

"There's a clearing over there." Eric pointed toward the trees behind them. "If he hasn't gotten here yet, that would be a good place to wait."

Again, Eric led the way.

"Why didn't we think to bring a flashlight?" Joy asked.

Lincoln was amazed at his sister's need to voice what everyone else was probably thinking.

The trees were thicker than the slope they had just climbed, though not nearly as dense as the downhill slope had been. A hundred feet in, the woods opened to a clearing eighty feet square. The awning of branches gave way to a canopy of bright stars.

"This is where we . . ." Gonzalez tried to find the right words. "This is where Adam shot at the bear . . . what we thought was a bear."

"The sheriff isn't here," Joy said, stating the obvious again.

"He must have fired the shots we heard." Lincoln gestured toward the woods to the south.

"I guess we need to head in that direction."

Serita sank to her knees. "I'm tired . . . Can't we just yell and see if he hears us?"

"Why not?" Baca agreed. He cupped his right hand to the side of his mouth and shouted.

"Sheriff Lansing! Can you hear me? Sheriff Lansing!"

All four listened for a response. After waiting a full minute, Lincoln made the same call again. Again, no response.

"Maybe I should fire my rifle," Eric suggested. "The noise will carry further than your voice. That might get his attention."

Lincoln nodded. "Sure. Go ahead."

The teen pointed his rifle upwards, angled away from the southern woods. He fired a single round. The sound echoed through the surrounding forest.

After listening for a moment and again being greeted by silence, all four began yelling.

"Sheriff Lansing! Sheriff Lansing! Sheriff Lansing!"

When they all quieted, Serita quickly asked, "Are we sure were on the right mountain?"

"This isn't a mountain," Joy snapped.

"Well, whatever it is, is this the right place?"

"Yes, it is." Eric confirmed as he raised his rifle. "Maybe if I fire another shot."

"What do you people think you're doing?" a firm, deep voice demanded from the darkness.

"Sheriff Lansing?" Eric asked.

"Yes." A man wearing a cattleman's hat and carrying a rifle stepped into the dimly lit clearing. "Who are you?"

215

"It's me . . . Eric Gonzalez. We met this morning."

Lansing stepped closer for a better look, then nodded. "Okay, Eric . . . What the hell are you kids doing up here?" He saw the rifle in Gonzalez's hands. "And what were you shooting at?"

The group could tell the sheriff was irritated at their arrival.

"I was just trying to get your attention," the teen argued.

"It's my fault," Lincoln said, stepping forward, irked at being called a kid.

Lansing looked at the young man burdened with a cast and sling. "Who are you?"

"My name is Lincoln Baca . . . I'm a wildlands firefighter from Santa Clara Pueblo."

"Did you get hurt fighting the fire?"

"Yes . . . well, sort of . . . I got hurt on Cerro Grande the first night of the fire."

"So, why are you here?" He looked around at the group. "Why are any of you here?"

"It has to do with the man who was chasing us last night," Eric interrupted.

"And that is?"

"It wasn't a man . . . at least I don't think it was a man. Not after what Lincoln told me."

Lansing looked at Baca. "What did Lincoln tell you?"

"That it was an *atosle*," Lincoln said. "The bear that walks like a man."

Chapter Seventy-Three

Lansing listened intently as Lincoln Baca described his encounter with the four creatures on Cerro Grande. To the Pueblo man, it appeared to be a family unit escaping the growing fire. He did not sense them as a threat. All they wanted was safety.

The term *atosle* came from his great uncle. In Tewa legend, they were large, hairy ogres that came from labyrinths beneath the mountains. Humans feared them because of their horrid appearances, but the creatures simply wanted to be left alone. That's why they were seldom seen.

"So, you think one of these *atosles* chased you last night," Lansing said to Eric. "Why would they do that?"

"I think Adam Sanchez might have shot one yesterday." The teen cleared his throat. "We thought it was a bear."

"You didn't check to see what you were shooting at? Was it still alive?"

"We don't know." He shrugged sheepishly.

"You don't know?" Lansing felt himself getting angry. "Your father should have taught you not to kill things for the sake of killing."

"It wasn't like that," Eric protested. "We were crossing the clearing to check." He pointed at the woods where the creature fell. "Then we heard something coming through the trees. It was loud and it was coming fast . . . None of us wanted to find out what it was. We just ran." He paused. "And I didn't shoot anything. It was Adam."

"Why didn't you tell me this morning about these . . . *atosles*?"

"We didn't know what was chasing us . . . We never saw it!"

"Why did you let me think men were after you?"

"I was embarrassed. I didn't want you to think that we were being chased by monsters."

"But it was okay for me to waste my time and resources. Is that right?"

"No . . ." the teen whimpered.

"Sheriff," Lincoln interrupted, "Eric screwed up. All right. Would you have come out here if they said a wild animal was chasing them?"

"I don't know," Lansing admitted. "I'd think about it first. I'd probably just send trackers out. They wouldn't have needed me to come along. I'm only here to make an arrest if necessary."

Lincoln gestured toward Joy. "When my sister told me about Eric and the others, I was sure what they ran into were the same . . ." He struggled to find a neutral term to use. "The same things I saw."

"What if they were? You still haven't told me why you're here."

"To stop you from killing them."

"Why would I do that?"

"If you thought a bear or a mountain lion was attacking people, would you do anything about it?"

"Well, sure."

"You'd shoot it if you had too, wouldn't you?"

"Here in the national forest, it would be a matter for the rangers." Lansing remembered the three teens were tracking a supposed renegade bear. "In fact, Eric, your father should have reported the farm animal losses to the district office. They should have handled this thing from the beginning."

Gonzalez knew the sheriff was right. He looked for a way to change the subject. "Where are the hunting guides that came with you?"

"I'm not sure." The sheriff didn't think he owed these intruders an explanation. "They got ahead of me."

"Tell him about the body!" Serita insisted, tugging on Lincoln's sleeve.

"What body?" Lansing asked suspiciously.

"We found a body on the canyon's other slope," Lincoln explained. "A man."

"Linc said he was attacked by a bear!" Serita said, wanting to be part of the conversation. After all, she was the first one to tell the sheriff about the dead man.

"A bear?"

"He was killed by some sort of wild animal," Eric added. "The way his chest was torn open, only something big like a bear could have done it."

"Who was he?"

Eric pulled a wallet and set of keys from his jacket.

"These were in his pockets." He handed the items to Lansing. "His name is Calle . . . Tito Calle. From Segovia."

Lansing nodded. It was too dark to read anything, so he was grateful for the information.

Even in the dim light, he could tell the two girls were shivering. "Okay, you found me. Now what do you plan on doing?"

"I guess we need to go home," Eric said.

"Do any of you have a flashlight?"

No one said anything. They just shook their heads.

"You can't climb up and down these canyons at night . . . even if you did have a flashlight. It's too dangerous." Besides, they needed to show him the dead body.

"I need to call my dad and let him know I can't get home tonight. Do you have a cell phone I can borrow?" Serita begged.

"Yeah," the sheriff said. He reached into a pocket on his jacket and felt around. It was empty.

"Dammit!" he swore under his breath. He checked other pockets to make sure his phone wasn't stashed in one of them.

"What's wrong?" Serita asked desperately.

"It fell out!" Lansing suspected it was lying on the slope he had tumbled down. He was positive it was gone forever. "Sorry."

"We're going to freeze to death up here!" Serita whimpered.

"Get a fire going," Lansing ordered.

The four gave the sheriff a blank look. No one had a lighter or matches.

"Start grabbing sticks for kindling. Bigger branches for the fire once we get it going."

"How much do we need?" Joy asked.

"Enough to get us through the night," Lincoln said, backing up Lansing's orders.

"Oh, good," Serita said. "You have a lighter."

"Not exactly," Lansing admitted. "But I do have a fire starter."

"What's the difference?"

"You'll see," he grunted.

Chapter Seventy-Four

After the long wait on the side of the road, Roberto and Juan Calle were hungry. Linda told them to watch TV while she warmed up a can of *Beef-a-roni*.

As the quick meal warmed on the stove, the worried wife called her mother-in-law.

"*Mamacita*, this is Linda. Have you seen Tito this evening?"

"*No, no. Not today . . . Why? He not come home?*"

"I haven't seen him since breakfast."

"*Did you call the repair place? Maybe he still at the work.*"

"No. The shop closes at noon on Saturdays. He said he was going to work an extra job somewhere."

"*Call him there then.*"

"I don't know where he went."

"*Oh-h-h. I see . . . I don't know then. Did you call Ramona? Maybe she know. Maybe Tito is with Jimmy.*"

"No, she doesn't know anything. We were together all day."

Linda told Emilia Calle about the accident. Her daughter and grandson were at a hospital in Santa Fe. No one was badly hurt, but they will need someone to pick them up so they can come home.

"*Ernesto can no drive at night. I not drive . . .*" Emilia's voice trembled with worry.

"I know," Linda said. Her voice cracked as she fought back tears. "If Tito was home, he'd go pick them up. But he's not here!" She cleared her throat. "I told Ramona to call me when they were finished . . ."

"*I talk to our neighbor,*" Emilia said calmly. "*He know Ramona and Tito since they were little. I know he will help. You not worry. You call me when she done at the hospital. Simon and Ernesto will go to Santa Fe."*

"Thank you, *Mamacita*! Thank you!"

Linda hung up the phone. Ramona and Jimmy, Jr. would be taken care of. The can of dinner was almost ready. After her boys were fed and bathed, they would be settled in for the night.

Then what? she thought. Wait for Ramona's call. Emergency rooms were slow. It could be past midnight before she called. That might be a good thing. Tito would surely be home by then.

But what if he wasn't? What if he had an accident too?

Almost everyone she knew had a cell phone. She thought it was an extravagance they couldn't afford. That night she admitted Tito needed one. It made sense. He could tell her when he would be home so she wouldn't worry. She could call him in an emergency . . . like tonight.

The thought that he wrecked their truck flashed through her mind again.

What will happen if we lost the truck? I can't go to the store. Tito can't go to work! What are we going to do?

She was immediately ashamed. Cars . . . trucks . . . they can be replaced. Her husband couldn't be. A fear washed over her. What if he didn't come home? What if he disappeared like Jimmy Clay?

She had spent the past few days worrying about Ramona. It would eventually turn out Jimmy Jr. would be fine.

But now she had her own desperate concerns.

Tears streamed down her face as she dished the children's food. She couldn't hold them back any longer.

Chapter Seventy-Five

The clearing was mostly exposed rock with little topsoil. The chances of starting a new forest fire were remote. The swirling wind came from the west. Lansing selected a protected spot near the trees on the northern edge of the stony meadow.

Eric and the two girls helped the sheriff gather wood. Baca sat cross legged, frustrated. He hurt. He had strained his broken bones to their limits. His body told him to sit and rest or else he would regret moving more than he already did.

Once Lancing determined there was enough material to build a good fire, he knelt. In the dim light he assembled pine straw, pinecones, and twigs for kindling. He found a piece of flat, pine bark.

His holster belt had four leather pouches . . . one held his handcuffs, two held spare magazines for his pistol. From the fourth he produced a buck knife. He made a pile of wood shavings for starting a fire. He then unzipped a jacket pocket and removed a thin, rectangular piece of metal.

The two females watched his deliberate actions with fascination.

"What's that?" Joy asked.

Lansing held up a three-inch-long object so they could see. "It's a magnesium fire starter." In the starlight it looked white.

"How does it work?" Serita asked.

"Just watch."

Lansing spent two minutes scraping shavings of the magnesium bar onto the pine bark with his knife blade. When he determined he had enough, he pushed the shavings into a nickel-sized pile. He scooted wood shavings and pine straw next to the pile for easy ignition.

He then turned the magnesium around exposing a black ferro bar, a kind of flint, imbedded in the side. Using the flat side of his knife, he deliberately and slowly ground the knife along the bar. A splash of sparks jumped from the bar onto the magnesium shavings. The shavings burst into a bright flash that burned at 5500° Fahrenheit.

As the pine shavings and needles caught fire, he added more and more twigs and pinecones. He moved back once the fire was sustainable and let the others build it bigger.

"Lucky you brought that," Lincoln said.

Lansing shrugged. "It's one of those things you stick in a spare pocket and forget it's even there. But you never know when something like that might be handy."

Eric and Joy were experienced fire tenders . . . Eric from camping . . . Joy from firing her pottery. Serita did as she was instructed. It wasn't long before they had a large, comfortable fire burning.

The smoke drifted to the east. Serita and Lincoln huddled together on the north side, their backs to the woods. Joy and Eric did the same on the west side. Lansing sat with his back exposed to the clearing, next to their stack of wood.

At first, there was little conversation. Everyone, Lansing included, realized they were thirsty, hungry, and tired.

Eric wasn't surprised when Joy voiced what the others were thinking.

"A tall glass of cold water would taste good about now," she said.

The silence was finally broken. The others felt safe to voice their wants.

"I'd be happy with warm water," Serita admitted.

"My mom's tamales would taste good," Eric chimed in. "She makes the best tamales in the world."

"I could take a hamburger," Lincoln said.

In response, his stomach growled loud enough the others heard it. Serita giggled.

After a few more meal suggestions, everyone grew quiet again. Lansing had said nothing during the discussion. Experience taught him talking about food or drink when you were hungry and thirsty only amplified those needs.

"Listen you three," Lincoln finally said to his companions. "I'm sorry about getting you into this."

Eric could barely keep his eyes open. "Nobody twisted our arms."

The two girls agreed. They were all volunteers.

"I'm still not clear why you're here," Lansing finally said, breaking his silence.

"I told you," the firefighter said. "To keep you from killing any *atosle*."

"You are not in the best physical condition to be delivering messages in this forest."

"I know that . . . now." Baca was annoyed at the observation, but the sheriff was right. "The reason I came out here is that it's my fault they had to leave Cerro Grande."

"How is it your fault? I thought the rangers from Bandelier started the fire."

"They supervised. It was the Black Mesa Wildland Firefighters, my crew, that actually started the fire. My boss thought it was being done wrong, but we did what we were told. Before we knew it, the fire jumped our fire line, and everything went to hell."

"I heard it was the wind that caused all the problems."

"Not at first. The guy in charge changed the ignition pattern. Our fire line wasn't cut for the new configuration. When the fire spread, our barrier wasn't sufficient to stop it . . . The wind kicked in after that."

"So how is any of this your fault?"

"I kept thinking about that family of *atosle* I saw. I couldn't sleep. I was worried about them. They weren't just animals. They were more like . . . people. They acted like they were human.

"The more I thought about it, the more guilty I felt about starting the fire that destroyed their home.

"When I heard about Eric and his friends . . . well . . . You know the rest."

"Yeah, I know the rest."

Lansing thought about Baca's *atosle* . . . large, ape-like creatures of the forest . . . rarely seen . . . to the point that most people didn't believe they existed. There were a dozen different names for these creatures in North America. *Atosle* was the newest for him.

The Cabrera father and son team popped into his thoughts. As professional hunters, they must have realized they weren't tracking a man. An obvious clue was what was left of Landa's German Shepherd. They knew exactly what they were after. Bringing such a trophy to the public would make them famous . . . even rich.

They must have thought he would have stopped them from shooting one. The Cabreras didn't want an argument about the ethics of killing such a unique creature. They had decided it was easier to eliminate him than it was to debate him.

He tossed four more sticks onto the fire. His companions were all dozing.

Without realizing it, he too started nodding off, lulled by the crackling fire.

Chapter Seventy-Six

The ranch house was dark when Tina brought the truck to a stop. Oscar Vega's truck was parked near the foreman's bunkhouse. A light was still on.

For all the time she spent shopping that day, Tina only had four items to bring inside. It took her and Marta two trips to carry all the English teacher's shopping bags into her little rental house. Gomez had made quite a hall. The explanation was easy. Marta needed a whole new wardrobe after she lost nearly forty pounds.

Turning on lights, Tina realized she was exhausted. It had been a very long day. It was unexpectedly made longer by the highway accident and the side trip to drop off Linda Calle and her boys.

Morales wasn't hungry. The two teachers hit a drive-through for coffee and a quick bite before leaving Segovia.

She wanted two things now . . . to take a shower and to talk to Cliff Lansing. She hadn't heard from him since noon. She tried calling him after the accident, but his phone kept going to voice mail.

Sitting on the sofa, she touched the redial button. A few seconds later, Lansing's phone requested her to leave a brief message.

"Cliff, it's Tina. It's ten o'clock. I wanted to let you know I made it home. Didn't want you to worry . . . Call me back as soon as you can. Love you!"

She hit the red "end call" button and closed the phone.

The chemistry teacher tried to reassure herself that Lansing was a big boy who could take care of himself. That didn't mean she couldn't worry about him. But good boyfriends . . . descent partners . . . were hard to come by.

She thought for a moment, then opened the clam shell phone again.

"San Phillipe Sheriff's Office, Deputy Barnes speaking."

"Hi, Sid, this is Tina Morales. You haven't heard from Sheriff Lansing this evening, have you?"

"No, ma'am. I have a note from the day shift saying he's tracking down some hombres near Polvadera. As far as I know, he's still out there."

"Okay." She could hide her disappointment. "If he checks in, could you ask him to call me?"

"Not a problem."

Hanging up again, Tina refused to consider that anything bad had happened to Lansing. He was in the mountains in a dead zone. There was no cell phone coverage. She couldn't call him. He couldn't call her. End of story.

After her shower, she lay in bed for a long time staring at the ceiling . . . telling herself over and over again . . . Cliff Lansing was all right.

Chapter Seventy-Seven

"What was that?" a loud whisper asked.

Lansing jerked awake . . . again.

It was impossible to sleep sitting up. He would doze just long enough to almost fall over. When he did nod off, he was jarred awake by the sense of falling. The ground was too rocky to lie down and there was no tree to lean against.

"What was what?" he asked softly.

"I heard a knocking," Joy Baca said. She sat, her back against a tree, Eric Gonzalez's head in her lap. He didn't stir.

"What kind of knocking?"

"Someone was hitting a tree. It sounded like they were using a stick."

Lansing listened. He was about to dismiss her observation when he too heard the knocks. Three of them . . . spaced a second apart. They came from the forest to the south.

"Is that what your heard?"

"Yes."

"Heard what?" Lincoln stirred. He had fallen asleep. He too leaned against a tree, Serita Silva's head on his lap.

"Someone's hitting a stick against a tree," his sister said.

"Are you sure?"

As if in response, there were three more knocks. This time, though, they came from the stretch of woods to the east.

"I heard them!" Lincoln said.

"Those weren't the same knocks!" Joy sounded worried.

"What are you talking about?"

"Those were closer," Lansing said. He stood and stared into the dark, his rifle in his hands.

"What should we do?" Joy asked.

"For now . . . nothing." The sheriff threw more wood onto the fire.

"Is that a good idea?" Lincoln asked. "They'll be able to see us!"

"They already know we're here." Lansing said definitively.

"Who knows we're here?" Eric asked, sitting up.

"There's somebody in the woods," Joy said. "We heard them knocking wood against trees." She looked at Lansing. "Do you think it's your hunting guides?"

"No!" Eric said before the sheriff could answer. "It's no hunters . . . at least not human."

"What do you mean?" Lincoln asked.

"We heard something hitting a tree yesterday . . . when Adam and I were crossing the meadow. It was just before that *thing* started chasing us."

"You think the *atosle* are doing that?"

"Yes, I do."

"Makes sense," Lansing agreed. "The sound of those knocks carry a long way. It's an easy way to communicate."

"Is it time to get up?" Serita sat up and stretched.

"No," Joy said, annoyed she would have to explain the tree knocking again.

"We need to stay alert," Lansing warned. "Just in case we have visitors."

"Who's going to visit us?" Serita whimpered, realizing she had no idea what was happening.

"Don't worry." The firefighter took her hand in his. "We have plenty of protection."

"How can you protect anyone?" Serita sneered, pulling her hand away.

The remark hit Baca like a slap in the face. The high school senior, only half-awake, was afraid . . . they were all afraid to one extent or another. But Serita's fear translated into a selfishness that precluded anyone else's safety. The remark was honest, though. In his present condition, he couldn't protect himself, let alone her.

The exchange did not go unnoticed by the other three. No one said a thing.

The other two seniors were angry at their classmate's callousness.

Lansing ignored them. He had more important things to worry about.

Chapter Seventy-Eight

All five stayed alert, listening . . . watching.

When a puff of wind stirred leaves or moved pine branches, imaginations took hold. When shadows moved, no one wanted to blame the flickering fire.

There were creatures in the darkness . . . creatures that wanted to harm them. Nerves were becoming frayed.

Whatever disdain Serita held for Lincoln evaporated under the strain. He soon found her cuddling next to him for protection. He obliged. The touch of another person was welcome under the circumstances. The reason for her unkind words earlier could be analyzed in the daylight.

An hour passed after the knocking stopped. The group began to relax. The threat seemed to be gone.

Eric was the first to fall asleep again. Sitting and leaning against a tree, his rifle slipped from his hands. Joy picked it up and held it as she sat next to him. She soon nodded off as well.

Not long after, Lincoln and Serita joined them.

Lansing kept watch alone, his back to the fire. He stomped his feet to help his circulation. He knew he couldn't sit. The temptation to doze off would be too great.

He tended to the fire. The stack of wood was dwindling. He knew it wouldn't last the rest of the night. He turned from the fire again, trying to determine the best way to gather more fallen branches.

Surveying the darkness . . . waiting for something to happen . . . something struck him in the middle of his back.

Lansing whipped around . . . his rifle ready to fire.

"What the hell?" he shouted.

His four companions stirred immediately. No one had sunk into a deep sleep.

"What's wrong, Sheriff?" Lincoln asked, struggling to stand.

"What happened?" Joy jumped up, ready to fire Eric's rifle if necessary. The other two teens stood as well.

"Something hit me!" Lansing studied the trees nearest him, expecting to see movement.

He allowed himself a glance at the ground near his feet. There was a baseball-sized rock he didn't remember seeing before. He looked back at the trees.

"Someone threw a rock at me!"

Eric reached for his rifle. "The *atosle*," he said. "Just like last night."

Lansing picked up the rock. "Like this?"

"No. The one that hit me was a lot bigger."

From the corner of his eye, the sheriff saw something fly by. Another rock, this time from the darkness of the clearing.

"Dammit!" Lincoln yelled as he stumbled backwards. Serita caught him before he fell.

"What's wrong?" she screamed.

Joy rushed to her brother. She saw a trickle of blood coming from his forehead.

Lansing turned again, his back to the fire. He pointed his rifle toward the sky and squeezed off a round. The sound reverberated through the meadow.

"What are you doing? Aren't you going to kill it?" Serita bleated.

"Not if I can help it," Lansing admitted. He added more branches to the fire.

"We need more wood." It was an order. He noticed the terrified looks on the faces of the three teens.

"Eric, you stand watch out here by the fire. Joy and Serita, you come with me."

"I'm not going into those woods!" Serita said.

"Fine," Lansing snorted. "In fifteen minutes, we can all just sit here in the dark! It's midnight. We'll be okay till sunrise."

"Come on, Serita," Joy ordered. "The sheriff has his gun . . . nothing's going to happen."

Lansing led the way. Joy followed.

Serita hesitated . . . until her classmate disappeared behind a tree. Afraid she'd get lost by being too far behind, she hurried to catch up.

Chapter Seventy-Nine

The forest was nearly as dark as a windowless room with no lights. The stars only occasionally shown through the leaves and needles. Searching for fallen branches by sight was impossible.

Lansing and the two girls used their feet to locate pieces of wood they could pick up. If the sheriff found something, he would notify the closest teen. He needed to keep his hands free for firing the rifle. He used sound more than sight to keep track of the two gatherers.

"Stay close," he ordered more than once when it sounded like they were wandering off too far.

"I can't carry anymore," Joy finally said. "We need to go back."

"Serita? Are you ready?" Lansing asked. When there was no immediate response, he yelled.

"Serita . . . Where are you?"

In response, Silva let out a scream. She was no more than ten yards away.

Lansing ran toward the scream. Joy dropped her bundle and joined him. In just seconds they ran into Serita running toward them. Joy threw her arms around her.

"What happened?"

"It touched me!" she shrieked. "I bent over to pick up a branch and something hairy brushed against my arm. A hand touched my head. It-it tried to get me!"

"Did you see anything?" Lansing pressed.

"No!" she said, her voice quavering. "It was too dark. I thought it was a tree . . . then it touched me! And it growled at me!

"Oh, God, get me out of here!"

Lansing took a step toward where Serita had been. He could see nothing. He would have sworn though that he heard footsteps heading away.

"Let's go back to the fire!"

"What about the wood?" Joy asked.

"Can you handle a rifle?"

"Yes."

"You can stand guard at the fire. Eric and I will get the wood."

***

"We didn't know what to do," Lincoln admitted as he wrapped his good arm around Serita. He was thinking of her as his girlfriend now and felt responsible for her safety.

"I'm-I'm going to be all right," she said, welcoming Baca's touch.

"What happened?" Eric asked.

"Serita ran into an *atosle*," Joy said. "It tried to grab her."

"Damn," the senior said. "What did it look like?"

The girl could only shake her head. "It was too dark."

"I felt its hair brushed against me . . . and I know it touched my head . . . with its hand," she said with a shaky voice. "It grunted at me!"

"You said it growled," Joy protested.

"Growled. Grunted. What does it matter?" Lincoln asked. "It scared the hell out of her."

"Eric, you and I need to get some wood," Lansing interrupted, handing his rifle to Joy. He pointed out the safety on the weapon.

"I'll gather. You protect us."

"Yes, sir."

The two men stepped into the dark forest. Lansing led the way, trying to guess the spot where Joy had dropped her collection of wood.

One hundred feet in, they heard a scream and Lansing's rifle being fired. The others yelled, "Sheriff Lansing! Eric! Come back!"

They ran to the clearing.

Lincoln and Serita huddled behind Joy. She held the rifle in a firing position.

"What happened?" Lansing demanded.

"Something came running at us . . . out of the dark," Serita whimpered.

"What did it look like?" Eric asked.

Lincoln shook his head. "It was a dark figure. It looked all black. It stopped when Serita screamed."

"I just fired the gun in the direction Serita pointed," Joy admitted. "I never saw what I shot at."

"So, you don't think you hit anything?"

"No, I don't think I did."

Lansing took his rifle back, ejecting the spent shell.

"What do we do now?" Eric asked.

"We stay together . . . Safety in numbers."

"What about the fire?" Serita whined.

Lansing's response wasn't encouraging. "It's going to burn out."

Chapter Eighty

Serita found a stick to push the embers closer together. The warmth of the fire disappeared. Hot coals glowed red, but no one else noticed as they slowly burned out. The others were watching the darkness . . . looking for any threat.

Three of the five now had weapons. Lansing had returned his rifle to Joy. He was armed with his 9mm pistol. Eric had his rifle.

With the fire extinguished, their eyes became adjusted to the star-lit clearing. No one talked. When Serita tried to whisper something, all four of her companions shushed her.

The only sound was from whisps of wind rustling leaves. The stress of the silence was grinding. All five jumped when the knocking started up again.

Three knocks came from across the clearing, spaced a second apart as before. Just a few seconds later three knocks answered. This time, though, these new knocks came from the trees behind them . . . no more than one hundred feet away.

Everyone turned their gaze in that direction.

"What should we do?" Joy whispered.

"Nothing," Lansing said softly. "Just wait."

"You should fire your gun again!" Serita insisted.

"They know we have guns." The sheriff kept his voice low.

After a long silence Eric asked, "How many are there, do you think?"

"Two, for sure," Lansing said.

"Why are they doing this?" Serita whimpered.

"I think they're trying to scare us," Lincoln said.

"They're doing a really good job," his sister agreed.

"We didn't do anything to them! Why can't they leave us alone?"

Serita was beginning to sound frantic. Lincoln held her even more tightly.

From the woods next to them came an animal sound . . . something between a grunt and a growl. It was no more than twenty feet away.

Everyone jumped in terror when Joy's rifle exploded.

"I'm sorry! I'm sorry!" She shrieked, dropping the rifle. "I didn't mean to do that!"

Serita leapt to her feet, about to run. Lincoln grabbed her. "Don't be stupid!"

"Pick that back up!" Lansing ordered. "And be more careful!"

"Yes, sir," Joy squeaked.

A short, gruff yowl came from the darkness of the meadow. The creature in the trees near them answered in a similar howl.

The obvious call and response told Lansing they were dealing with very intelligent beings.

"I think they're toying with us," he observed. "Like a cat plays with a mouse."

"What do you think they'll do?" Eric asked.

"Hopefully, nothing if we stay together."

The *atosle* in the clearing snarled loudly. It was closer now. Its partner snarled as well.

A six-foot log easily weighing a hundred pounds sailed through the air from the open meadow. It landed with a thud on the remains of the fire sending up a splash of sparks.

Serita screamed.

Joy shrieked, "It took my gun!"

Lansing kept his gaze on the clearing. "What happened?"

"A big hand came out from nowhere . . . it grabbed the gun out of my hands!"

"Eric, did you see anything?"

"No, Sheriff!"

"Joy, are you okay?" her brother asked.

"Yes." She scooted closer to Gonzalez.

From the dark forest, the *atosle* let out a series of triumphant whoops. Its partner responded with a loud yowl. Then from the woods came a loud thwack of something hard slamming against a tree.

"I believe I just lost a rifle," Lansing said grimly. "Be ready, Eric. I think they've finished playing."

A crash of splintering wood erupted from the far end of the clearing. Accompanying the sound was a roar louder than anything Lansing had ever heard before.

"What new hell is this?" he muttered.

Chapter Eighty-One

The roar rumbled through the clearing for a solid fifteen seconds. To the humans it seemed even longer.

"That thing sounds pissed!" Lincoln said when the roaring stopped.

"At us?" Serita sniffled.

The *atosle* in the meadow let out two, loud but short yelps. From the trees near them came a quick whoop, followed by something storming through the woods toward them. A dark figure easily six-foot tall jumped out of the trees and ran through the knot of people.

The move was so quick and the night so dark that no one could have given an accurate description of the creature.

No one was sure what would happen next. Lansing and the others had to use their imaginations to picture what actions were taking place no more than one hundred feet away.

The *atosle* that had roared let out a series of loud, angry whoops and growls. To Lansing it sounded like a tongue lashing. That guess was fortified when two other "voices" whimpered submissively. There were two whacks that sounded like slabs of meat being slapped, each followed by a loud yelp.

An argument of sorts broke out. The two *atosle* that had attacked them were defending their actions. The sheriff could see them in his mind, pointing in the direction of the people, holding their hands in a "What else were we supposed to do?" Pose.

Lansing remembered the description of the four lumbering forest dwellers that Lincoln Baca had given. He sorted out the actors. The two attackers were the "children" of the group. They were being admonished by a parent . . . probably the patriarch. He couldn't help but marvel at how "human" the entire scene played out.

One of the siblings would plead their case. The father would respond with loud rebuff. The other would offer their defense. The father would counter the argument with another vocal slam.

The debate continued to rage as the three began moving away toward the far end of the clearing. The arguments grew fainter and more distant. Their sounds diminished to nothing as the *atosle* family withdrew deeper into the forest.

The darkness was soon wrapped in silence.

Chapter Eighty-Two

"They're gone!" Joy finally whispered.

"No kidding," Lincoln snapped . . . tired, sore and impatient with his sister's predilection for the obvious.

"What should we do now?" Eric directed his question at the sheriff.

"Find some pinecones and leaves . . . see if we can resurrect our fire," Lansing instructed. "It's safe for us to gather wood now. No use being cold if we don't have to."

***

The coldest part of the night seemed just before dawn. Possibly, Lansing thought, because a slight breeze had picked up. The fire had dwindled to practically nothing. He saw no point in adding more wood. They would be leaving their camp once everyone stirred. There was no shovel or water for dowsing flames. The best they could do was spread the coals apart.

The chirping birds helped awaken the others. It didn't take much since no one really slept deeply. Everyone grumbled about being thirsty, hungry and dirty.

"My suggestion is let's head for your car," Lansing said. "We can get water and maybe a snack at the Phillips station in Artiga."

"I need gas, anyway," Serita said. After she stood, she offered her hand to Lincoln to help him up. The two smiled at each other.

After the rollercoaster of emotions through the night, Lansing suspected their relationship might be stronger now. Maybe not in the long run. Young love was fickle. But for now, they seemed to be heading in the right direction.

Before leaving the area, Lansing took a quick look in the woods, hoping to retrieve what was left of his rifle. He didn't waste much time looking. There were other priorities. Besides, he would be returning to the area soon. He needed to find out what happened to the Cabreras.

The sky brightened considerably by the time they reached the edge of the canyon. The glow of the Cerro Grande Fire had disappeared. The sun was no more than a white orb, its rays poking through the ever-present column of smoke.

"If you want, I'll go first," the sheriff offered.

"That's all right," Eric said. "We know how to tackle these slopes now . . . to make it easier on Linc."

"Lead the way, then."

Eric resumed the zigzag pattern he established the day before. The trip to the bottom of the canyon was mostly uneventful. Lincoln Baca nearly lost his balance at one point. Lansing rushed to help, but Serita waved him off.

"I've got him!" she insisted.

The rest of the way down she stayed close to Lincoln to provide any assistance he needed.

When they started up the opposite side of the canyon, Lansing asked Eric if he could remember where the body was. Gonzalez had made mental notes about where to find Tito Calle. He knew the authorities would need to recover the man eventually.

Again, the two girls kept their distance as Lansing inspected the body. To Eric, Calle looked the same. There had been no scavenging by coyotes, racoons or anything else.

"We guessed he was killed by a bear," Eric said.

The sheriff nodded but said nothing. He was forming his own opinion, however, it had nothing to do with bears. For public consumption, though, he wouldn't argue against the bear theory. He made his own mental notes on how to locate the body. He would lead the recovery party . . . maybe even later that day.

It was 9:30 by the time they exited the woods near Serita's car.

Lansing couldn't help but notice the shiny, new tire rims strewn about. He picked one up for closer inspection, marveling at how light it was.

"We saw a couple more in the woods," Eric said.

"Really," Lansing responded.

"Yeah," Lincoln added. "We have no idea how they got out here."

"I have a good guess where they came from," the sheriff said. He saw no point in discussing the Western Auto theft. It didn't involve any of his companions. He set the rim back down.

"Where is the dead man's truck?"

"Just up the hill from Serita's car," Lincoln said, leading the way to her Citation.

Lansing continued up the hill. He tried the key Eric handed him the day before. It unlocked the door and started the engine. Satisfied he would not have to crowd into the little hatch-back, he shut off the engine. He had spotted the derelict barn further up the hill.

"Sheriff! We're ready to go!" Eric called.

"One minute!" he shouted.

Lansing hurried up the hill. The barn doors were still open. As he grew closer, he saw the paneled truck. The truck's rear doors were open as well. Inside, were three stacks of rims like the one he inspected a few minutes earlier. He also saw dried blood where it pooled on the floor.

"Well, Sheriff," he said out loud. "Looks like you solved a crime . . . just like a nut finding a blind squirrel!"

He closed the doors to the truck, then the barn doors. Pointing the truck down the hill, he followed Serita and the others. Lansing knew he could find his way to Highway 15 and Artiga eventually. It was easier to simply follow someone who knew the way.

Chapter Eighty-Three

Lansing paid for Serita's gas, bottles of water, breakfast burritos and coffee. The clerk behind the counter was kind enough to loan her personal cell phone so calls could be made.

"I'm fine, Mom," Serita promised. "I'm in Artiga with Sheriff Lansing . . . No, nothing happened! I was with Joy Baca the whole time. I'll be home in half an hour, forty-five minutes tops."

Joy made a similar call to her mother, as did Eric Gonzalez.

Lansing made two calls. The first to Tina Morales assuring her he was all right. The second to his office. He would be in later, but he gave the dispatcher a heads-up about the dead body the kids stumbled upon the day before.

Serita, Joy and Lincoln went home to Santa Clara. Lansing drove Eric back to his family's farm. He would make arrangements to have Calle's truck retrieved later.

Albert Cabrera's Explorer still sat where he parked it. That told Lansing the father-son team were still in the mountains somewhere.

"Listen, Esteban, if those two trackers show up to get their SUV, could you give me a call?"

"Sure, Sheriff."

"And if they ask where my Jeep went, tell them one of my deputies came and got it."

"Okay. Can I ask why?"

"Those two SOBs left me for dead in one of the canyons. I'd like it to be a surprise when I arrest them personally."

The farmer smiled and nodded. "That won't be a problem."

***

"You're a mess!" Tina said after giving her man a welcome home kiss.

"I probably feel as bad as I look," he admitted.

She followed him to the bedroom.

"You're going to lay down for a bit, aren't you?"

"Can't. Too much going on."

After he showered and while he dressed, he gave her an abbreviated recap of what happened. Tina felt the back of his head where he had been hit.

"I can feel the bump! Are you sure you're okay?"

"Okay, enough."

"Why are you putting on civilian clothes?"

"I learned my lesson about hiking in mountains in my uniform." He paused as he laced up his boots. "I think I found out who robbed the Western Auto."

"Oh?"

He told her about the dead body in the canyon and the tire rims near the man's truck. Tina's eyebrows knit with concern.

"His name wasn't Jimmy Clay, was it?"

"No. Who's Jimmy Clay?"

Tina told him about the car pileup the evening before, assuring him his beloved truck was fine. The driver of the car she almost hit, Ramona Clay, hadn't seen her husband since Tuesday. She was afraid he was dead.

"No. The man's name was Tito Calle."

"Oh, no!" she whimpered.

"What's wrong?"

Tina gave a more complete explanation of what happened, who was related to who, and how. She had even driven Linda Calle and her two children home. The mother was worried her husband wasn't back from a job he was working.

"My God, do you think I should call her?"

Lansing shook his head. "That's not the kind of news you spring on a loved one over the phone."

She nodded sadly. "You're right . . . how are you going to tell her?"

"In Albuquerque, when we had to report that kind of bad news, we called it a 'death knock.' It will either be me or one of my deputies."

The schoolteacher fought back tears.

"Would you like me to fix you something to eat?"

"Maybe a sandwich-to-go and a thermos of coffee, if you don't mind."

"You know I don't mind," she said, giving him a kiss.

Chapter Eighty-Four

It was noon before Lansing made it into his office. As per usual for a Sunday, it was nearly empty. Deputy Barnes manned the dispatch and phones.

"Who's on patrol today?" the sheriff asked, looking at the duty board.

"Jake Redwine and Ray Blanco. Deputy Trumbull in forensics is on call. I gave her a heads-up after your call this morning."

"Good man . . . I'll be in my office if anyone calls."

The next few days were going to be hectic. The San Phillipe Sheriff's office was the chief law enforcement unit for the entire county, even in the national forests. Lansing knew his office didn't have the resources to retrieve Tito Calle's body, as well as search for the Cabreras. He had his differences with a few of the Forest Service managers in the past. However, he hoped the Santa Fe National Forest Rangers could provide vital help with those two problems.

Looking at a resources map, the Cerro Grande Fire only affected the Segovia District of the Santa Fe Forest. That was the same area he needed help. The district office was being manned twenty-four hours a day during the fire emergency, but the director was currently out.

Lansing explained his situation. The ranger taking the call assured him the director would return his call when he could.

The State Police said they could supply a helicopter to extract Tito Calle provided the body was moved to an open area. The sheriff agreed. First, he needed help to move the man from the canyon slope to the top of the mesita.

Cohino Valley Ambulance service had a team available. They could bag the body and move it. Lansing arranged to rendezvous with them in Artiga at 3:00 p.m.

Deputy Marla Trumbull would join him there as well. He wanted her to pull prints from the paneled truck. She also needed to get a blood sample from the back to compare with the blood found behind the Western Auto. The sheriff was positive it would be a match, but it needed to be checked just the same.

***

The two EMS workers grumbled about climbing up and down the steep slopes. They were a bit placated when they discovered the body only had to be moved to the flat area above the canyon. After Lansing called the State Patrol on a borrowed cell phone, he released the ambulance people. They didn't need to wait for the helicopter to arrive.

Trumbull called him on his cell at 5:30. She was finished with her work. He released her as well, knowing she would have to deliver her samples to the Santa Fe forensics lab in the morning.

The helicopter arrived at 6:30. The crew was instructed to take Calle's remains to the State Medical Investigator's office in Albuquerque. He handed them the paperwork he had filled out at his office earlier.

It was after eight before he got home. He was tired, hungry and ready for another shower. Before calling it a night, he made one more phone call.

"Hello, Esteban. Sheriff Lansing. Did Albert or Ray Cabrera show up to get that Explorer?"

"No, Sheriff. It's still sitting out there. I haven't seen either one."

"Okay. Thanks."

As he closed his eyes, he couldn't help but wonder what happened to those two experienced trackers. He had honestly hoped they had found their way back to civilization. He had already had his fill of trekking through the forest.

It would have been so much easier to arrest them at their homes!

Chapter Eighty-Five

Eric and Joy sat together at lunch. After getting to their respective homes the day before, they didn't call each other. They had both been depleted physically and emotionally.

"Were your folks angry that you spent Saturday night in the mountains?"

"No." Eric shook his head. "But I think it was only because the sheriff drove me home.

"He took responsibility for us spending the night out there. He said Linc needed to find him. By the time we did, it was too dark for us to leave. They didn't ask what went on and I didn't tell them. Neither did the sheriff."

"Why not?"

"If I told them some sort of monster attacked us, my mom would never let me leave the house again. Besides, both of my folks would want to know what it looked like. I never saw one!"

"Yeah . . . none of us did . . . I didn't see Jerry Landa this morning. Is he still in the hospital?"

"Yeah. He's getting operated on today. They're putting pins in his ankle."

"Wow. Is he going to make it to graduation?"

Eric shrugged. "What did your folks say about Saturday night?"

"Nothing, really. Mom was more worried about Linc hurting himself again. I don't think my dad even knew we were gone. He's been busy with that stupid fire. Have you told anyone what went on?"

"Yeah, Adam Sanchez. I told him to keep it to himself."

"Will he?"

"Yes," Eric said emphatically. "This all started when he shot that "bear" . . . and he knows it."

***

Lincoln Baca wanted to tell Uncle Eluterio about Saturday night. By the time he got home Sunday, though, he was too tired to walk to his uncle's house. Besides, he hurt.

The Santa Clara Pueblo Senior Center was closed on the weekends. He had to wait til Monday morning.

Pauline Baca asked what happened in the mountains. Neither of her children wanted to discuss the details. Lincoln only admitted they found the sheriff. He told him about the *atosle* and asked him not to shoot any. They only stayed the night because Sheriff Lansing said it was too dark to hike out.

Pauline's motherly instincts told her something did go on. Whatever it was, she knew Joy would fess up eventually. Lincoln would never crack. He was good at keeping secrets.

***

Eluterio Tafoya was thrilled to see his nephew again. They both sipped on coffee served in disposable cups as Lincoln recounted Saturday night's encounter.

The elder pueblo man listened intently. He asked no questions while Lincoln talked, though he nodded often. When Baca finished, his uncle raised an eyebrow.

"You never saw them?"

"Just the one who ran through us . . . but it was dark, and he ran so fast we didn't get a good look."

Eluterio stared out the window for a long time digesting the information. After a while, Lincoln started to say something, but his uncle raised his hand to silence him. He wasn't finished thinking.

Finally, Tafoya said, "You were attacked by *atosle* who have not learned the importance of avoiding people. I think they made their father angry. If you had been hurt or killed, others would come to hunt their kind and destroy them. The father knew this."

"How did he know what they were doing?"

"The tree knocks. The sound can travel for miles. You said the sheriff fired his rifle . . . as did your sister . . . The parent could easily suspect what his children were up to.

"He intervened before they were killed . . . or they killed a person."

"What will they do?"

"They cannot return to Cerro Grande. The father knows they cannot stay here. They might have a memory of the rivers to the north. I would think they would want to return there."

"That's over a hundred miles from here. They could do that and not be seen?"

The uncle nodded. "I do believe they can . . . and will."

Chapter Eighty-Six

"What are you staring at?" Tina asked.

"This is where we found Ray Cabrera's body." Lansing pointed at a brown-stained area a few yards away. "That's where a large amount of blood had accumulated."

"You thought that was Albert's blood, didn't you?"

"We all did. After two weeks of analysis, the crime lab can't say for sure what it is. It wasn't Albert's blood. All they said it was ninety-seven per cent human."

This was the sheriff's first trip into the national forest since the search had been called off two weeks earlier. He was only there because Tine Morales wanted to see where he had his encounter with the *atosle*.

***

The search for Ray and Albert Cabrera began in earnest on Monday, May 15th. Up to thirty men and women, a mixture of Forest Rangers, law enforcement and volunteers, participated.

Ray Cabrera was found the first day . . . a mile from the clearing where Lansing and the others spent the night. He had been shot in the back. The large splotch of blood a few yards from the body was still reddish. The searchers assumed the blood was Albert's. That changed the searchers' approach. Judging by the amount of blood, they were convinced they were looking at a recovery rather than a rescue.

Scenarios were proposed. The most popular one was the two men were attacked by other hunters and left for dead. Albert managed to crawl away and died somewhere in the forest.

The search lasted for eight days, suspended the Tuesday before Memorial Day weekend. It quickly became apparent the only person that would miss either father or son was Bess Cabrera. She had to accept the idea that her son's body might never be found.

In those weeks since Lansing's encounter with the forest dwellers, other tragedies unfolded in San Phillipe County.

Tito Calle's death was determined to be caused by a wild animal . . . most likely a bear. No actual forensic evidence was found to definitely say it was a bear, though. The Medical Investigator could only surmise the type of animal by the size of the claw marks. A single red hair was found, but it was decided it was most likely human left by EMS personnel during transport.

The crime lab in Santa Fe found the blood in the stolen paneled truck matched the blood collected at the *Western Auto*. One enterprising technician went one step further, matching those two samples with the body found east of Artiga. It also matched traces of blood found on Tito Calle's knife.

Lansing could only conclude Calle was both a thief and murderer.

Tito Calle and Jimmy Clay had been joined at the hip since high school. They were even brothers-in law. It wasn't much of a leap to guess the body Lansing and Deputy Trumbull recovered belonged to Clay. Ramona confirmed the keychain found on the body was Jimmy's, ending the speculation.

The two men had a falling out. Tito killed Jimmy and dumped the body. For Lansing, that was the most logical interpretation. That was what his report would conclude. More significantly, that was what he told the grieving wives. He informed them separately, unsure of their reactions. He had no idea that, in the long run, the friendship between the two only grew stronger. Both women knew Tito had saved his sister and nephew from any more misery.

The Cabrera situation was more problematic. Before reaching the top of the mesita, the sheriff remembered hearing a single gunshot. Seconds later, there were several shots.

Before writing his report, he interviewed his four companions from that night. What did they remember?

Both Lincoln and Eric did hear the same gunshots. Eric, however, added one more piece to the puzzle. Not long after the final shots he heard a scream. After that, nothing.

Ray Cabrera's autopsy confirmed he died from a gunshot wound to the back. The medical examiners, however, estimated Cabrera only had hours to live before he was murdered. He had a brain hemorrhage, probably from a fall. His behavior would not have been normal and would have gotten more erratic as the bleeding continued.

Lansing remembered how subdued Cabrera was when they met at the Gonzalez farm. As the day progressed, he got moodier and more secretive.

Ray finally snapped, attacking Lansing and leaving him for dead.

Bess confirmed her husband's unusually positive mood that day. She kidded herself that he had changed. She also attested to the fact that Ray was thrown from a horse the day before. The hemorrhage must have been from that fall.

***

Lansing felt there was a common denominator that linked Calle's death, Cabrera's disappearance, and his own experience on the mesita . . . the *atosle*.

Lincoln Baca had said his uncle told him about the ancient forest creatures. The sheriff asked if the elder Tafoya would speak with him. He had questions.

At first, Eluterio refused . . . either because of the old man's distrust of law enforcement or white men in general, Lansing guessed. Finally, Baca convinced him the sheriff's intentions were honorable.

Eluterio provided his insight into what he thought transpired.

Adam Sanchez shot at what he thought was a bear. It was, in fact, an *atosle* . . . the mother or one of the children. The creature was not killed. If it had been, those boys would never have made it out of the forest alive. They were, however, chased by the father . . . driven from the woods.

Lincoln described the patriarch as being over eight feet tall. He could have overtaken the teens at any time. If he had done them harm, other hunters would have followed. The Landa's dog was killed only because it attacked the *atosle*.

Lansing and Eluterio both agreed the only reason the sheriff and the others weren't killed was because the father intervened. Why they were attacked would have to remain a mystery. However, what happened to Tito Calle would have been their fate as well.

The blood found near Ray Cabrera's body belonged to an *atosle* the hunters probably killed. The scream Eric Gonzalez heard was most likely Albert. His fate would have been as bad as Calle's, if not worse.

Whatever happened to the two missing bodies . . . Albert Cabrera and the dead *atosle* . . . would remain another unsolved mystery.

***

"Have you finished all of your reports?" Tina asked as they hiked to the truck.

Lansing nodded. "For the most part.

"What did you say about those *atosle* creatures?"

"Nothing."

"Nothing! Why?"

"For starters, I'm not sure anyone would believe me. Besides, I told Eluterio Tafoya I wouldn't."

"But you saw them!"

"I never did. Something ran through our camp that night, but I can't describe it. I heard a big commotion in the dark, but that's it. I heard something. I saw nothing!"

Epilogue

June 6, 2000; noon.

The same day Lansing made his return to the mesita in the Santa Fe Forest, state and federal officials announce the Cerro Grande Fire had been contained. It had taken nearly five weeks to bring it under control. Up to that point it was the most destructive wildfire in New Mexico history.

Forty three thousand acres were burned.

Four hundred lost their homes in the town of Los Alamos. Over one hundred and twenty buildings were engulfed at the National Laboratory. Portions of Santa Clara Reservation, Bandelier National Monument and the Santa Fe National Forest were consumed.

The Cerro Grande Fire was not declared completely extinguished until July 20th, twelve weeks after it started.

One thousand firefighters were employed to fight the blaze. It was impossible to determine the loss to wildlife, but no human fatalities were reported.

***

There was a quick knock on Sheriff Lansing's open office door. He looked up.

"Good morning, Marla. What's up?"

"I took a weird call last night," Deputy Trumbull said. "Roberto Rodriguez claimed he spotted three large, hairy creatures crossing his property. He swore one was nine feet tall."

"Yeah, Bob's ranch is next to mine . . . He hadn't been drinking again, had he?"

"Oh, I don't know, sir. He did seem upset, though."

"Did you look around?"

"Yes, but I didn't see anything . . . I was curious . . . Do you think he really saw something?"

Lansing let out a long, slow breath. "I really doubt if it's anything. Make a note in your duty log, but I wouldn't lose any sleep over it."

After Trumbull left, the sheriff turned his gaze to the window.

"Well," he said under his breath. "Uncle Eluterio was right. He said they would try to find their way north."

Coming 2022!

MONTEZUMA'S FIRE
A Sheriff Lansing Mystery
Book 11
By
MICAH S. HACKLER

The establishment of a Native American Reform Church in San Phillipe County draws immediate controversy.

A former Wildlands Firefighter searches to find a new purpose for his life.

State and national elections campaigns are underway.

Sheriff Cliff Lansing finds his hands full with a series of bizarre murders on his hands.

For more information
visit: www.SpeakingVolumes.us

Coming Soon!

WALKING RAIN
A Howard Moon Deer Mystery
Book 8
By
ROBERT WESTBROOK

Inspired by true events, *Walking Rain* is a tale of corruption, international crime, and the challenges of parenthood as Howie finds himself an unexpected father to a teenage girl.

For more information
visit: www.SpeakingVolumes.us

Coming Soon!

"ASTONISHINGLY CLEAR TELLING OF THE AMERICAN WEST"

LAKOTA
COWBOY

THE NOVEL INSPIRED BY TRUE EVENTS

JOHN HAFNOR

**For more information
visit:** www.SpeakingVolumes.us

Sale!
SPUR AWARD-WINNING AUTHOR
PATRICK DEAREN

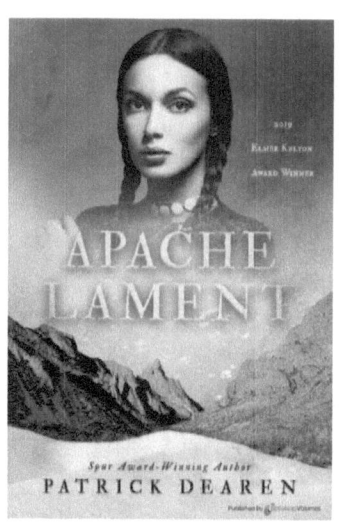 

For more information
visit: www.SpeakingVolumes.us

On Sale Now!

AWARD-WINNING AUTHOR
MARDI OAKLEY MEDAWAR

For more information:
visit: www.SpeakingVolumes.us